The Storm Witch.
© 2019

The "Storm Witch" is based on a true story from early 1600s, many of the characters are real, likewise the island of Westray, one of the northern and most populated Orkney Islands, is very much a real location.
However, much of the story is embellished with my own interpretation of events and therefore reads as fictional.
I do not intend to offend and offer my apologies should you believe any of the characters have been portrayed incorrectly.

Molly Mack

Chapter I

Janet sat up with a start, slightly disoriented as a shard of morning sun shone through the skylight. She had lain, half asleep, watching the whole scene play out before she made to open her eyes. "Dreams are scary, so real..." she said to herself jumping down from the box bed, her bare feet clapped on a cold stone floor. Hopping onto the foosty rag mat was no help, it was equally cold but also damp. "Shit" Janet whispered as she tiptoed onto a pair of old dungarees lying in the corner and wriggled into her old grey working dress which wasn't very becoming, however was practical and would have to wait a while yet before washing despite its smell and stains.
She pulled on big leather boots over socks that looked more darned and patched than original sock. "It's so cold in this old house I'm sure the mice left long ago in search of a warmer bed" she mused clumping her way through the passage, laces untied, to where her dad had fallen asleep in his chair as he did most nights.

Smoke billowed into the room as Janet stoked the embers of last night's fire and placed two lumps of precious coal on top of a few low-grade peats, the flames rose and the hanging water pot began to sing. "Well I say dream, and if you want to be picky" she said to old Jock, "I had been asleep, however it was so real, the smell of rotting seaweed still hung in the air this morning and I could hear the silent mumblings from a group of men as they stood around looking at three bodies on the beach".

"You and your premonitions lass" old Jock said, "stop worrying, it's a fine morning, the sea is as flat as the loch o' Swartmill and the boys'll have another grand day at the fishing. Pour some water into me cup and get me a bannock and a bit o' cheese fae the press…if you have a blink tae spare" he added.

The door clattered shut before he could finish his sentence and Janet breezed past the window with Salty jumping excitedly at her heels. Janet's old dog was called Salty, which was short for Salted Herring. Salty earned his name from his constant habit of rolling amongst everything rotten, especially on the beach. Last years salty brine that fishermen tipped out of their bait barrels onto the beach to make room for the new seasons catch was the probably his most favoured.

"Don't be making a fool of yersel' again lass" Jock shouted in vain as he hoisted himself onto wobbly legs "come back here and tend to your old faether, I could do wae a hand".

In northern Scotland, summer days are long and darkness lasts only a few hours, for the tenth day in a row a cloudless sky over the island of Westray promised another calm and peaceful morning. Shoals of haddock were being caught this season off the Noup in quantities not seen for many years and larders were full. The warm settled weather had been ideal for salting, curing and drying fish for winter stocks.

Davo and Ben, or as they teased their mother, David and Benjamin being their Sunday names, were up as soon as daylight appeared over the horizon and spirits were high as the brothers walked from Gill, the small stone cottage overlooking the Sand o' Gill where the Garrioch family had lived for generations. Sheep scattered as they crossed the field, leaving silvery patterns in the morning dew. One final day's fishing would be salted down in barrels for winter creel bait and the boat hauled out for a month or so to be repaired and painted in preparation for the harvest lobster fishing.

Davo and Ben joked about Tam as they drew closer to Quoygrew where the boat was kept in a purpose-built noust. They could see him in the distance pacing back and fore, cap pulled over his ears, eager to get off to sea. It was like this every morning; Tam arrived first, sorted out bait, checked over the sail, put the nile in the bottom of the boat and generally prepared everything for the day ahead. Patience was not one of his attributes and often declared "the boys" deliberately arrived late just to annoy him.

Tam was in his usual agitated morning mood, shuffling around sorting out the already sorted things, never able to look them directly in the eye he would "voo on" as the old folk would say; as soon as they came in hearing range he started to complain and true to form came out with one of his standard rebukes "Come on boys hurry up, where have you been?... Up most o' the night I wad think, debblin' in the eel kirn... Any man can sing and dance at night, but it takes a real man to get up to work in the morning".

"Ach, you never stop moaning min, it's easy to see how you earned the name Greetan Tam." Davo jested as they both grabbed the gunwale and began to heave the dinghy down the bank.

Tam fell silent as together they balanced the boat upright and guided her down towards the water's edge aided by Ben inserting and removing short wooden planks repeatedly under the keel to smooth the journey over jagged rocks. They had been working together for three seasons now and could have performed this launching process in the dark.
Ben and Davo said no more to agitate the situation when Tam was in a poots with his head hung low, however they knew his mood wouldn't last long and the air would lighten once they got afloat and underway. Tam's ability as a fisherman was second to none and was a good mentor, his frequent lack of humour was therefore tolerated and respected.

Gentle rippling waves advanced slowly around the boat and the stern began to lift as they walked back up the shore to collect fish baskets, oars, sails and other bits and pieces including, essentially, bread cheese and milk.

Ben stopped suddenly hearing his name called, turned sharply and losing his balance, skited along the green slimy seaweed-covered rocks, arms wind-milling and fell hard on his bottom. Davo roared with laughter and Tam wore a seldom seen grin, as he carefully picked his own way up the shore with exaggerated caution.
Ben looked up and recognized the silhouetted shapely figure; "Janet, what on earth are you doing here lass?" He said scrambling up the bank to where she stood, out of breath wiping strands of hair from her tear covered face. "You gave me a fair flix, what's wrong?"

"Oh Ben, I'm so glad I caught you. Something terrible is going to happen. Please don't go to sea today, it's no safe, you are in great danger".

"That's a mighty statement, what danger is there? A finer morning tho'll never see. Nothing's going to hurt us the day. In fact, if Tam had packed more food I wad ask thee tae come for a sail as it'll be the last trip for a while."

"Let me sit a minute and catch me breath…I ran the whole way here fearing the boat would be long gone." Janet sat on the low tangle dyke and Salty jumped onto her lap.

"Down dog, go and fetch a rabbit or something" Ben flicked his ear and shoo'd the smelly dog away, Janet was taking deep breaths and trembling a little as Ben lowered his voice, "Tell me more…what ails thee lass?"

"I had this vision… you ken, like the time peedie Finn was stuck in the peat hill… The three of you were lying stretched out on the sand, everyone was staring. They just stood there, looking, pointing and whispering as the flood tide crept up the beach towards your feet. Ben, you were dead, all three of you were lying there dead.
You know how it is, things I see sometimes happens, this time I know it will, it was so real. Please don't go to sea Ben, you can come help me clip sheep at Vere the day instead."

Tam was standing down on the shore looking up at the pair, not amused, "Janet Forsyth, you are a fine lass and I'm happy our young Ben has teen thee a liking, I believe thoo might shape up to be a fine wife someday, however at

6

the risk of falling out…us men have work to do and are wastin' precious time stood here watching a lovers tiff, the tide is turning and we need to be off."

Davo and Tam walked down to the water's edge, "Come on boys" shouted Tam, "We'll be off." He lowered his voice… "Bloody weemin, steer clear Davo boy, nothing but trouble" He turned and waded up to his knees in the cold water, slung a canvas bag onto the thaft and clambered aboard.

"Aye Tam" Davo said, "Thoo should ken, on to thee third wife."

Ben took Janet in his arms, glancing over his shoulder he wondered if a kiss would be too daring in full view of Tam and Davo, their elevated position on the bank felt a bit like a staged play. "My dearest Janet, you worry too much, I ken you have what the old folk call a sixth sense, it's a bit scary I admit and I don't want to chance fate. I am so confused, I love you dearly and I hate to see you so distressed, however It's such a bonny morning, there is no sign of the weather changing for days, I have that old cork float you gave me on board the boat and promise to keep it close just in case…I will be careful. It's the last trip of the season, we won't be long away so come down and give us a hand gutting and cleaning the fish when we get back. Tam usually organises a couple of jugs of ale on the last night, so if it's anything like last year old Jock P and Sammy will appear wae their fiddles and it'll be a fine night. We can spend the whole day together the morn, Sunday is the day of rest and we will make the most of it, promise."

Tears streamed down her cheeks as their lips met. "I know something is wrong Ben, I just know…. It wasn't a dream.. it was too real…please take care, come back safe….."

Janet stood watching the rust coloured sail shrink into a tiny dot as the ebb tide carried the tiny craft towards the nor'western horizon. She turned and walked home with a very heavy heart.

A big black horse was tied to the fence as she approached the four pillars and Salty barked at the imposing figure of Thomas Trail leaning against the high stone wall.

 "A fine morning Janet, what brings you out so early?"

"Just don't bother me Mr. Trail, I need to get home."

"You might want to take yon thing under control Janet" he said pointing at the growling dog. "It wouldn't last long in my care with an attitude like that".

"That 'thing' is a dog mister Trail, I believe him to be a very good judge of character" Janet replied with a steely stare and called Salty in to heel. "I can only assume he has met you before and has good reason to be on the defense, normally he wouldn't hurt a fly."

"Ah yes, your dog seems to be headline gossip around the island, however I believe old Reverend Hutton is not going to pursue his complaint."

"Aye, he won't make any more noise because it will highlight his clandestine activities, he'd have to explain what he was doing on the shore below Vere at midnight."

"You might be right lass, I for one would like to know what the old thing was up to, especially at his age, he's no too good on his feet… but I warn you, keep that noisy dog on a piece of rope because others might not be so well disposed". The Laird turned and strode up beside Janet as she walked on, "I think I'll walk a bit, your company will be welcome."

Janet didn't slow her pace, "No thanks mister Traill I'd prefer it if you didn't."

"Look, I'm just interested in the welfare of my tenants, I need to know how you're coping with the croft, your dad's illness has left him very poorly I hear."

"Sorry, I'm not trying to be difficult" Janet said warily, looking up at his square-cut jaw line, he was a handsome man she had to confess to herself, in another life she may have been attracted. The Laird, who lived in the big house at Skaill was known to have a foul temper and was treating his tenants very badly, seven families had been evicted last winter to make way for sheep farming and it was rumored he was looking for excuses to move out more.
"Thank you for asking, my dad indeed is not very mobile these days, we are coping and he will improve with rest. However, this is not a good time to talk, I need to be on my way."

"So when is a good time, tonight perhaps? I could come past and write off some of that unpaid rent"

Janet caught her breath, this was not a healthy direction and she could sense a smirk on his face without looking up, "You are not welcome at Vere Mr Traill, well you ken it."

Thomas Traill strode on behind Janet in silence for a couple of minutes. "Is that Benjamin and his brother out with Tam at the fishing?" he enquired, glancing back over his shoulder towards Noup. Without waiting for an answer he went on;
"They work hard and they've had a good season. His dad left the family a fair sum of money I believe, the boy must be worth a few pounds now.
His pot of gold won't last long if he shacks up wae the debt-ridden Forsyth family I'm afraid, he might be well advised to steer clear".

Another few seconds passed as they walked in silence. Thomas Traill's eyes were narrowed, watching her body sway and bouncing ponytail ahead, "I think you better watch your back Mr Traill" Janet replied at length with a quiver in her voice, never raising her gaze from the grass track ahead, "You are not a popular figure and there are people in this community who do not like what you, John Balfour and some of the other landowners are doing to the island."

The leather booted tall figure stopped, hands on hips "I am flattered you feel a need to warn me Miss Forsyth, I take that as a complement. Give your father my regards but do not forget to remind him that my patience has expired and rent is due next month." He had to raise his voice as Janet stomped onward without acknowledging his threats. "Health or no health you need to pay for your patch on this earth...nothing for nothing Miss Forsyth" was the parting shot Janet heard as she hitched up her frock and splashed across the burn, muttering oaths and words she didn't realise she knew.

Chapter II

Jock was back in his chair asleep when the door slammed shut, he sat up with a start, "The Laird's on the warpath dad, I guess we should sell off the last twa old ewes to help pay our debts, looks like we have to do something this time he's not making good noises this morning I doot.."

"Ah! Janet lass I'm just a poor old thing, no worth the space I take up...me legs are useless, I can't help with the harvest, I have no secret pennies stashed for a rainy day...I'd be better off joining your mother."

"Och faither, don't speak like that, there's a lot of life left in that old bones yet, thoo'r no much over sixty and on the mend. Plenty rest will sort, tho'll be fine in no time. It's been a good summer at the fishing and Ben will help get the stooks in, we'll get things back on course in no time".

"We can't rely on him to carry us through another winter lass, he works hard and he'll burn himself out...we might as well sell the twa yews indeed, no get much for them I doot as their lambing days are over". Jock paused a while and looked up at Janet as she busied herself with the boiling pots hanging over the open fire. I would readily agree if Ben asked for your hand in marriage, a move doon tae Gill would be the making o' thee. There's plenty room for another wife in that hoose....his mother sells baking to the shops, another pair o' hands would be fair welcome I would guess."

"Awa wae thee fether" Janet scowled "I'm no ready for marriage yet and anyway, don't think for a minute I'll up and leave thee cooped up here in Vere alone. We'll manage. We can have a right think about things when cousin Anne comes nort for twa days in October, she's a sorter outer. So wheesht and forget aal your nonsense."

The door burst open with a bang and Salty jumped from his nest, Janet caught the barking frightened dog mid-air as he launched himself towards the sudden intrusion. "Janet, am I glad thoo'r here, come quick" Mary o' Bigging gasped as she held on to the door and tried to regain her breath. "wir young coo is in a right poor state, thoo'r so good wae animals and we can't afford tae lose another…can thoo come an help lass?"

Without a moment's hesitation, Janet picked up her old straw basket, ran to the press and grabbed a couple of fattie cutties a jug of ale and her headscarf. "I won't be long dad, this snack'll keep me going for noo, I'll dig up twa tattie shaws tae boil up for tea when I get back."

Mary and Janet sat on damp straw in the middle of the darkened building, a couple of small skylights enabled muted shards of low-level daylight into the tiny cow shed. Janet was tired and cold, she could hear a skylark singing high above the stone roof and knew it was still only early evening. Wrapping the old knitted shawl tighter around her shivering shoulders she drew her legs up and leaned her chin on the cold wet dress covering her knees. It had been a messy birth and everything was stained and messy however the tiny red calf was making a healthy slurping noise as Mary held its head and spooned heavy creamy milk they had taken from the mother cow into the receptive mouth. "Beesmilk is what it needs…pour on as much as it will take for now, It'll soon be up and feeding on its own" Janet said in a distant tone.

"This bonny peedie calf wouldn't have survived without thee help Janet, I couldn't have done it on my own… such a gift…. Thoo kens we don't have much to live on and to lose wir only calf this year would have been devastating, thanks ever so much. I'll take along some beremeal and a grain o' milk the morn for thee dad….."

Breaking a long silence Mary looked into Janet's eyes "Thoo kens they call thee The Witch" she said cautiously.

"….doesn't bother me" Janet responded at length, however her bowed head indicated differently, a tear rolled down her cheek. "You find those who do most of the shit stirring don't have much between their lugs. Good God, the so-called witchy things I do is just common sense…old family remedies, handed down over generations.
I'm no different fae them wae all their fancy education. I sometimes think we are being deceived by doctors and ministers… they don't want common folk like us to ken what they do or how they do it…my guess is money, the root of all evil…money…"
Janet paused and watched the light from the skylight above begin to dim.
"I learned a lot fae me mither, she was so good wae remedies, she would brew up what she called her 'potions'; nettles, dockans, sooros, hawthorn, whins tangles and loads more. Everything that grows has its purpose for being here, each and every plant exists for

more reasons than we will ever ken......I wish I knew more about how to use all of nature's gifts, such a pity to lose this knowledge. I should have paid more attention to what she was showing me... Poor mither was taken away all too soon I doot, all the potions under the sun couldn't help her in the end."

The pause was long and Mary knew she shouldn't interrupt Janet's monologue and waited.

"The minister hasn't convinced me that Christianity will bring peace and happiness to everyone and he doesn't like me supporting the ways of the past. The doctor doesn't like anyone even suggesting they might have a cure for an ailment that didn't come from one of his expensive bottles...aye it would threaten their very existence if I could call on all the remedies my old ancestors used....."

"Aye lass I believe thoo'll no be far wrong, the old folk used to have a cure for near any ailment.
I heard the minister say something last week that worried me though" Mary whispered, "He was telling the congregation that anyone who interfered with the work of the Lord were servants of the Devil; if God wanted a lamb to die, then you should let it die, do not interfere...it is Gods Will."

"Who does he think he is, jumped up "sooth mooth Bible thumper...he adapts those written words to suit his own selfish ends. It appears to be all right to run and get the doctor to help if he chaps his finger or Mistress Minister needs medicine for her gout. That's the same thing, its altering Gods will if you call the doctor isn't it?"

"Aye, I agree lass. Thoo kens what he's like though, he picks on folk that are fragile and he seems to have it in for thee. The more thoo does tae help others, the more he twists it into something that will get the community on his side. I wouldn't trust the big lump o' lard as far as I could throw him."

Another long pause as the calf slipped down into the hay and lay within licking reach of its exhausted mother.

"I believe he was openly asking the congregation last Sunday to report unusual activity and suspicious behavior. It worries me Janet.
They tell me he wants tae leave the island as soon as the Kirk finds him another parish. However he's getting old and he's no in the best o' health any more…they'll probably keep him here out of the way until he retires. Or expires, she added with a snigger. "so just keep thee heed doon and hope he the latter happen first."

Chapter III

Janet lay on her bed exhausted, staring at the wooden planked ceiling of the old box bed, still fully clothed. The day had been very long; on returning from the calving she had dug up a shaw o' tatties and washed them in the burn beside the shed. Her father had been lying on the floor when she arrived home, having lain a few hours he was very cold and confused. A cup of warm milk and honey had warmed him up and was now sound asleep in his chair.

The evening was engulfed in a thick damp fog which was worrying. Fog was a fisherman's nightmare; without the sight of land it was all too easy to become disorientated and with notoriously strong tides around the islands the combination was a bad mix. Ben said they would be back home on the flood, which ended three hours ago.
The long summer daylight was dimmed with the heavy mist and Janet decided to go down to the shore to see if there was any sign of the boat.
She still had last night's premonition of the washed up bodies of Ben, Davo and Tam imprinted on her brain and felt her pace quicken as she got nearer to the noust.

"Oh my God!" Janet shouted as she came over the banks; the fog was lifting over the sea and Noup Head cliffs were magnified through the haze, creating a dramatic back drop for three men standing silently on the beach. Looking out to sea and she stumbled down the rocks and ran towards them, "I told them not to go, I told them something would happen…. I knew something would happen…."

"What you speaking about Janet?" said one of the men as he turned around, "What do you ken that we don't"

Sensing hostility towards her comments Janet replied "I ken enough to be worried when the fog comes in."
She was feeling physically sick with fear and worry, unable to contain herself a raised pitch voice erupted from inside as she glared back at three pairs of scrunched-up eyes; "They're no back yet and they'll no be back…I warned them not to go, somethings happened to them, I just ken….."

"A grain o' summer mist and Janet here has them devoured by the sea serpent….." Oliver Howison chided and they all laughed.
"Tam is a good seaman and kens the tides like the back o' his hand" he said, "they probably won't come back until morning as the tide has turned and the ebb will hold them out there most o' the night. There's no wind to fill the sail and I'm pretty sure they have no intentions of rowing all the way home"
Ignoring Janet he turned to the others "I guess we'll have to wait another day for Tam to pour out his newly brewed ale… ya coming back for a jar at the inn?"

They all turned together and strolled up the beach, kicking limpets off rocks, glimpsing back at the lone silhouette on the shoreline and mumbling to each other without offering her another moment of their time.

Every morning for the following couple of weeks at least two dozen islanders had walked the clifftops, searching

bays and geos on the west side, gazing seaward for clues to the disappearance of the three men and their boat. However, nothing was ever found.
The weather had then unfortunately broken with strong westerly winds putting an end to the bounteous fishing and the searches scaled down to a few hardy souls, including Janet, who walked up to Noup Head every day, however after too many rain-soaked experiences they also ceased.

Suspicion and gossip was alive in the community as to the fate of an experienced crew on a flat calm sea. The favoured rumour was that Janet and Ben had an argument and she put a curse on him and the rest of the crew. She had some violent clashes with locals and there had been worrying activities around Vere during the dark autumn nights. Janet heard noises outside and shed doors were left open, amongst other concerning incidents the barly kiln was contaminated and had to be dumped, robbing her and her father of much needed winter food.

The intimidation stopped when Janet's father died two months later, however she became detached from the community and was seen less and less by her neighbours. Depression led to her becoming increasingly inward and reclusive during a harsh northern winter that took hold of the islands. The only people she saw during this dark period was Mary o' Bigging and her childhood pal Bob.

Janet had proved her worth in years past as a youngster helping her father at the fishing, gaining the respect of other fishermen despite being female. Her unconventional attitude and clothing at the time raised many eyebrows, however were tolerated as she could out fish many of the older salts. Since the loss of Ben and her father she again took to wearing old fishing britches, to the disgust of the few who saw her out and about. "Most inappropriate clothing for a woman" was the common retort. The minister was even known to refer to her attire in his weekly condemnations from the pulpit.

Janet spent many long dark nights of this first winter alone cold and hungry.
Repairing the old boat, with grateful assistance from Bob became a necessity, not only as a desperate aim towards addressing her hunger problems but to save her sanity. Many hours were spent packing hemp between old clinker strakes and plastering on a good layer of tar inside to ensure the gisened hull would not let in too much water when launched. The sails were old and fragile, however were taken home and sewn up as best could be achieved with limited resources.
No animals were left on the croft to create an income and no crops were harvested to pay the rent. Ebb meat, as the islanders called limpets whelks and the occasional crab became her daily diet with an occasional small redware cod or ceuth caught when the weather was good enough to launch the dinghy. A few neeps and kale survived the winters gales in Vere's plantiquoy which Janet knew was essential to include in her limited diet.

There came a point where she was so low, having never eaten for days she was weak and lay on her bed, cold, wishing she could just slip away and join Ben.

Bob walked in one day with a huge jug of ale and a basket of food. "Janet Forsyth, if your mother could see you now. I do not believe she would recognize the wreck you have become. Get your arse out of that nest and sort yourself out. I ken I'm being coarse…so would you wae me if the tables were turned. You are a young intelligent woman and there is a big world out there, you have an obligation to the Forsyth family, you need to start now…First you eat a fill o' mutton and bunnos, I won't leave until you do, then we share this jug of ale…"

After her worst hangover in years a turning point had obviously been reached, thanks to a most devoted friend.

Janet became increasingly adventurous in her hunt for food and determination returned whilst still keeping a low profile in the community. She could be seen sailing alone and further offshore in the early morning light of summer. The tiny boat was returning with increasingly good hauls of fish and her expertise and daring was rapidly becoming the local talking point.
Weather never seemed to be a problem, "The stronger the wind the sooner I get home" she would say. Bob was always a support and there to help drag the old dinghy back up the beach on her return, no matter what time of day.
Catching bigger and better fish her diet began to improve along with her income.

Her ability to handle a boat would have gained more admiration had she been a man, however worrying rumors were being created and circulated; tales of collusions with the sea gods, serpents and fairies who lived beyond the shores would keep the fireside ale yarners going well into the night. Whenever someone lost a net or broke an oar Janet was a very convenient source to blame. The most concerning and potentially dangerous development however was the Reverend Hutton's increased accusations regarding her "healing gift with animals and collusions with sea serpents"; he was now openly accusing her of witchcraft and was recruiting others onto his campaign.

Janet was aware of the growing hostilities and once more drifted into an increasingly less communicative state, her reclusive lifestile helped deepen suspicions within this deeply naive and religious community.

Chapter IV

Dark clouds gathered on the western horizon and a cold bitter wind whistled through holes where simmans bound the roof thatch together, "just another job to add to a growing list for next spring" thought Janet. So much to do, the old house is falling apart, I don't know what mither would have thought about it all, she was much stronger, she never gave up....well, she did eventually, but her illness was cruel and painful, no-one deserves to go that way.
"I wonder how long I can stick it out" she found herself ask old Salty in a whisper, afraid of waking him as he had finally stopped looking for attention and lay tightly curled up on a rug in the corner.
"This is just so unbearable, it soaks every last grain of life from my bones, just being here, alone and cold. I wonder what might lie beyond these barren shores for the likes of me if ever I could pluck the courage to make a move to the Mainland, "the big flit" the islanders call it".

Her quiet sobs could not be heard over the raging wind and winter noises outside, "No education, no money, nothing to sell, what future can there possibly be for a barren spinster and her three legged dog...."

Janet's teeth chattered as she lifted the lid of the old kist, where winter woolies were kept; the large wooden box was the only place safe from the infestation of field mice looking for a winter nest. She gathered out an old jumper her dad once wore and in front of two flickering candles opened a seam with a pair of rusty scissors and began to unpick the stitching bit by bit. Swollen cold hands made the task of winding delicate yarn difficult and slow, however Janet was really keen to re-use this particular wool, partly because it had been lying unused in the kist for years but mainly because North Ronaldsay wool was valued throughout the islands as one of the warmest and best wools money could buy.

Her dad had been so proud of this jumper having earned it many summers ago for his bravery and help during a fateful day when one of the creel boats belonging to the neighboring island of North Ronaldsay had foundered losing one of their strongest fishermen.

Janet's dad, Jock was not a regular fisherman, however had been invited to join the local boat "Maggie Jean" on a trip to the fishing grounds off Fair Isle as they were a man short. The Maggie Jean was a fine boat, built in Westray to similar lines as the local skiff, with larch planks salvaged from a wreck on the north side of the island. She measured five feet longer and a foot deeper than anything else in the north isles and had proved herself over many fishing trips to be a fine able sea boat, her only downside was that she was heavy to row and even heavier to haul up the beach. Her mast was fashioned from a Canadian pine yardarm and the lug sail was made from light canvas washed ashore from the same wreck. At nineteen foot long the Maggie Jean was a big boat by any standards and the pride of the Westray fleet.

This particular midsummer trip had enjoyed good winds and copious haddock and even some ling, only two days out they were heading back home with 30 baskets. Maggie Jean was carrying more than she probably should and sat low in the water, rolling heavily over a long swell. An occasional wave topped over the gunwale making the south west passage wet and uncomfortable for the crew as they hunkered into their oilskins, catching up on some long overdue sleep between frequent baling of the bilge. The sky was clear with a brisk northerly wind sweeping them on a course closer to the island of North Ronaldsay than skipper Jimmo would normally have taken, however the tide would turn soon and lift them towards the east side of Papay on the final leg home to Westray.

North Ronaldsay lies on the far north east corner of the Orkney Islands with a particularly grim reputation for shipwrecks; when the seas are rough the low-lying island becomes very difficult to see from a boat and combined with strong tidal currents many lives have perished on its rocky shores. The moon at this particular time of the month was "maakan", as the old folk called it, meaning tidal heights were greater and currents becoming stronger. Danger is never far from the mind of an old salt like Jimmo Craigie, occasionally standing up and scanning the world around as far as his failing eyes could see. Maggie Jean rode another crest, carving the white-topped swell in two and progress was steady in the now quiet surroundings where a few hours ago the crying gulls had been creating their noisy aerial display fighting over discarded fish guts.

Jimmo rose to his feet and grasped hold of the fish baskets stacked two high, steadying himself against the pitch and roll peered into the distance, pipe firmly clenched between tobacco-stained teeth; "get yer arses off the tulfers boys" he hollered "luks like somebody's in trouble ower bye the point".

The dark brown sails of a small boat were flailing wildly in a freshening breeze, they could see some activity on board, however the boat was clearly out of control.

"Do you see what's happening?....the boat's being swept towards the skerry, there's someone aboard and It'll be the end o' them if they get in among yon breaking water. I'll steer over and sail as close as possible, be ready to drop the sail and have the oars ready to run out when I say".

He didn't need to shout, the three men jumped from their lairs, although half asleep the tone of Jimmo's voice put them all on high alert within seconds. Without question spray sheets were rolled up stowed away and ropes dug out from the fish-smelling bilge. Retrieving oars from under the heavy, tied-down baskets was not easy in the lumpy motion. Time was ticking past rapidly as Maggie Jean bore down towards the stricken boat, Jimmo asked for the sail to drop "Slow her down boys, we're going too fast, get the oars out...hurry, hurry".

Despite digging two big blades deep into the sea they were swept past the stricken boat with seemingly unstoppable momentum. Jimmo turned the helm hard to starboard and as she made her slow turn in the swell a wave spewed green over the gunwale and into the bilge. Maggie Jean rolled onto her beam ends as Jock clambered up the windward side and held his breath for a very perilous and heart stopping few seconds before she came back upright, head into the wind and a ton of cold water sloshing amongst the baskets of fish. Jock scooped water over the side with an old canvas bucket like he had never scooped before while Davie and Bill fought the sea in tandem sweeps of the heavy wooden oars. The boat's increased weight made it difficult to regain control as the long paddles dug into frothing waves, however with strength and determination in charge they slowly but surely inched ahead and progress was made back out against the wind and swell.

"Still too far to leeward" shouted Jimmo, "get ye'r backs into it boys, get her away outbye further, row like the Tanglie Man was biting your heels, row for the lives o' that poor souls".

Two men could be seen in the water, one had his arm slung over the stern of the dinghy and a young boy was in the boat, holding on to one of them in the confused sea alongside. The boy was plainly struggling to keep the man above water whilst trying to free the sail halyard with the other hand.

"Hurry up, I can't hold on much longer, for God's sake hurry" the boy was heard yelling as Maggie Jean inched further and further away.

Jimmo was aware that with the wind now stronger, a rescue that didn't endanger themselves was getting increasingly unlikely, if they managed to get alongside the stricken boat it would be impossible to use the oars and the risk of being swept together onto the rocks was a high possibility. He voiced his fears to the crew as they heaved in silence on the oars, making good distance back out to open water.

Jock was having the same worry and met Jimmo's eyes, wiping spray from his face with his water sodden hat he looked back at the still flailing sail; "I'm going to swim across and lend a hand, keep the boys rowing far enough away up wind to make a safe turn, hoist the sail and bear back down towards those poor buggars, keeping your speed up."

"Don't be daft" Jimmo shouted, "You'll never make it in this sea".

"You said it yourself; we can't get alongside or it'll be the end of both boats, we need to do something now or it's all over for them lads. As you come back down towards us under sail steer near enough to throw me the heavy tow rope, turn her on a beam reach as you pass, and head out towards the east, it'll give you the speed and power to pull us clear".

Jock took off his boots and jacket and rolled over the gunwale into the sea as the Maggie Jean climbed up a swell that seemed as high as her mast, leaving the others no alternative but to row like the Devil himself were breathing fire down their necks. The developing situation was more scary and worrying than Jimmo had ever experienced, he threw the pipe from his mouth and yelled to the crew.

"This is it boys, that headstrong bastard has left us no choice, it's all or nothing now, keep her moving out another cable yet, when we are ready I'll turn her as fast as I can, you'll need to hoist the sail bloody smart as she comes about".

Jock was a good swimmer, however under the conditions it seemed a long way to the dinghy; the sea was bitterly cold and his woolen clothes weighed him down deep in the water making an already difficult undertaking a very serious mission. It took a long time to make headway over the swell that had now developed with the turning tide and swallowing salt water every stroke made it very difficult to keep focused on direction. Pure determination and as Jock declared later, a thick head, enabled him to eventually thrash his way through hells gate to arrive alongside the boat, numb with cold and out of breath he made a grab for the green painted hull and hung there gasping for air, Jock was fully aware another half dozen feet would have been too far.

His impulsive jump into the sea had increased the odds that death was on the agenda for someone today and there was every chance that he was now within minutes of joining this boats crew in a watery grave.
With one arm hung over the stern Jock found he couldn't move, his head reeled with exhaustion, the world was in a spin and he froze. His brain said move, but his body was seizing up, if he didn't do something right now all would be finished, no second chances, time was not on his side.

The young boy's voice was at panic level now and Jock was brought right back to the unfolding predicament, he made another determined effort and with one big push lunged toward the man alongside, one hand still holding on to the boat he lifted the drowning man's head out of the water. With his grip relieved, the boy leaned inboard and came back with a rope, wrapped it under the deep floating arms of the now motionless man and tied it to a cleat, he dropped the flailing sail and clipped the halyard on to the rope and began to heave. The man was very heavy and unable to help himself as they struggled a long while without any gain to get him back into the boat.

Jock took a risk and lunged upwards with a final effort and rolled himself over the low gunwale and into the boat as a wave slid past, bringing another barrel sized lump of water in with him. Pulling himself up on his knees Jock got positioned alongside the boy, which, given the combined weight tipped the dinghy over at a dangerous angle.

"He's gone" the boy cried out, "I can't see him anymore, he was hanging on to the stern, faither's gone….".

"Look back here" Jock shouted, "grab a hold and help me lift…."

Heaving together and with a great final effort they rolled the man in, assisted by yet another wave, which were getting more common as the the rocks became increasingly close. Jock moved his weight over to the far side as the shivering man spewed out gallons of water and sat upright in a depth of bilge water. "Looks like you'll make it" Jock shouted to the man as he wrapped a rope around his waist and tied him to the centre thaft. "Just sit there and don't move".

"Luk yonder" cried the boy as he was bailing water, the Maggie Jean appeared riding a white wave under full sail, oars splayed out like mallimack wings. She was bearing down at speed with the wind behind, someone shouted as a rope flew uncoiling through the air and fell across the stern of the dinghy behind Jock, he turned with flailing arms and held on as the rope came tight. The burning sensation was fierce enough to hurt through cold numb white flesh, however he held on with an iron grip, nothing would make Jock let go at this point as he put his back into the strain and waited with grim determination for the next wave to sweep the boats nearer together. The blood stained rope slackened in his hands and stumbling over the man in the bilge he lunged towards the mast, wrapped it a couple of times around and tied a knot the crew would have called a farmers hitch and waited. "No time for any fancy ropework" he thought, "I just hope it holds".

The tow came fast like a crack from a gun and Jock ducked instinctively fearing it had parted, Maggie Jean lifted on the next wave and the rope remained tight with the full weight of both boats fighting the elements. The stricken dinghy's bow was pulled around swiftly and both began to move away from the boiling cauldron. Slowly at first then gaining momentum they left the skerry behind with literally feet to spare.

As they turned towards the jetty under tow the boy shouted over the boom of waves and white spume
"Faither, faither are you there faither?"
Jock took the bucket from the boys hands and bailed out water as fast as he could.

The whole population of North Ronaldsay had witnessed this unfolding drama from the shore, tragically unable to do anything to help. The loss of young Tom's father was a disaster for such a small community, however it was also appreciated that the crew of the Maggie Jean had saved two others, averting an even greater tragedy. The Westray fishermen were treated as heroes and spent the night ashore in warmth and drank ale until early hours. Before sailing home next morning they swopped a basket of fish for a couple of freshly killed sheep and Jock was presented with a woolen jumper for his selfless actions and bravery.

"It's the warmest gansey I've ever owned" Jock would say every time he hauled it out for winter use. "I'll never forget that poor boy the day he lost his faither though. It's a tough life out there on North Ronaldsay, you think we have it bad here Janet, but believe me out there it's no' a life, it's a penance. We can survive here in Westray a winter without supplies from the Mainland, we have neeps and ither greenery growing out in the plantiquoy and plenty of cockles and spoots on the beach. North Ronaldsay doesn't have a sheltered bay nor even a decent beach to haul up boats, so fishing is limited in the winter. They can be cut off from the rest of the world for months at a time when the wind blows. Naa it takes a special kind of soul to survive out there, no me, I wouldn't last a winter……"

"Believe me bairn," he would moan on, "I wonder why they bother when it's easier somewhere else, that peedie island is no better than old captain Rendall told us about Cape Horn, "That God forsaken place at the other side of the world should never be viewed by mortal men" he used to say "I should ken, Staten Isle kept us prisoner for over three months when the "Cynthia" foundered there in '86. Nothing to eat but scorries and limpets…and that was the middle of summer be damned."

Chapter V

Janet wound up the last of her wool into a ball and placed it beside the knitting needles. "Aye, Captain Rendall, limpets, I ken what that's like.....Struggle struggle sleep. Struggle struggle weep." she repeated over and over. "Bob was right, I can't waste away my life here any longer, the island is full of bloody minded, cruel selfish people who make it their life's ambition to cause misery and despair for others. Whatever happened to that community spirit the old folk spoke of, gone forever I'm afraid. The lairds are causing disquiet among our island crofters with false accusations and harassment, they raise the rents to a point that no one can afford, tenants are driven away to make room for bloody sheep".

"Well," Janet stood up and said aloud, startling Salty, who jumped towards the door, "you self-centered, money grabbing race of human depravity you have made your point and can say goodbye to the one you call the witch, the blot on your island is going away. There are employers in the south crying out for workers and pay good money for willing hands, I have a brain and I have decided to use it. My cousin fled to Edinburgh two years ago and is doing well in that fine big developing town. It is long past time I made a move. As soon as I find some ink and dry parchment in this old house I will write back and accept his offer to give me a room. A fresh start it is Salty, decision made, I doot though you might have to stay, I hear they eat dogs in cities.".

Janet reversed out the low doorway, ducking her head under the wooden lintol as always and pulled her collar up

against the horizontal rain. turning towards the shed a movement caught her eye and she stopped.
Salty ran in circles making low growlie yelps at the figure approaching through a gap in the stone wall. Janet relaxed as she heard Bob shout "Come quick, come on across to the banks, there's a ship in distress oot nort, looks like they might be coming in Papay Sound, she looks well beat up with her sails all tattered".

Slipping and sliding down the steep clay bank they could make out a few shapes on the shore, shoulders humped against the north wind; James Craigie o' Brough, Oliver Howison o' Waal and Thomas Rendall o' Rackwick stood huddled together, fingers pointing towards the sea. White foam and spume blew across black rocks as the howling wind increased, creating an image of drifting snow. The stark picture was like a stage set as the drama unfolded less than a mile away; beyond the Aikerness skerries a large cargo boat with only one small foresail flying could be seen wallowing and running before the wind, a huge swell had built up between the islands and things did not look good...

"Slow down Janet" shouted Bob, "You'll break a bloody leg if you don't ease up".

"Oh my god Bob, look" Janet shouted back against the piercing wind, "Her tops'ls have been carried away, if she's been through the Boar on the north end o' Papay she's lucky to have survived at all ....she's turning, she's turning this way, towards us, towards the shore."

The northerly swell was now boiling through the relatively narrow channel between Papay and the Holms, sweeping the large boat in a ponderously rolling gait before the wind. Heavy with cargo her decks seemed more below the sea than above as the lumbering vision rose again out of the trough, she heeled over dramatically onto her larboard side at the same time as the wind blew an extra couple of knots. Turning. Slow at first, her huge bowsprit began to sweep around and gained momentum as she lay on her beam ends, almost ninety degrees across the wind. The beach onlookers could see green copper sheathing on her undersides as the big hull rose again, she lay at an impossible looking angle as another scream of icy wind ripped through the rigging. "She's broaching, she's broaching" the figures on the rocky beach were shouting and jumping as the massive hull rolled her gunwales under and the lower yards ripped through the mountainous swell.

"Thank you God, please God, we've had no wrecks for many years, we need this so much, oh thank you" James Craigie was calling out skywards.

"You shameless old scrounger" shouted Janet over the howling wind "There are men on board that boat with wives and bairns. You need to be praying for your God to save them, not for your pockets to be lined in the name of misfortune".

"You mind your lip young witch, you are not welcome here". James raged back "Go on home to your peedie hovel by the Knowe and get on wae your knitting, like all good wimen should be doing on a day like this...might still be time to earn yersel a reputation as an eligible bride for some misguided tinkler".

"You are an evil old belkie James Craigie". Janet snarled, moving away from the anger, "Ignorance is no excuse for such a forked tongue."

Against the piercing spray Janet scrunched her eyes together and peered through an old woolen scarf. She could see the menacing sea curl green over the ships gunwale and along her deck as the large black painted hull continued to sweep westwards towards the onlookers on the shoreline. To Janet's relief the dark shape continued turning, turning until her bows pointed north and the bow rose again like a great whale out of the foam. White water streamed from her scuppers, the ship slowed right down, rolling more gently and came to a stop in the relatively calm tidal eddy to the south of the skerries. Some frantic activity could be seen up for'ad and within seconds the anchor disappeared from the rail, the rode came taught and she settled, anchored, head to wind.

"Oh my God" Janet cried, "she's anchored up, what on earth will they do now?"

"She's holding, the anchor's holding, they'll be ok." cried Bob.

"Oh! Bob, just listen to the haaks on the shore, they are still waiting for the pickings...they all ken she's fine for the moment under the lee of the skerry, however, when the tide turns in a couple of hours combined with this huge wind against the spring ebb tide it will be a maelstrom. I've seen the seas here many times, it is not a good place to be anchored. The wind is rising and the rocks will claim another victim before dawn if they don't move, Oh Hell Bob, come with me, come on we have to do something".

They ran back towards the old shed at Vere and stood just inside the doorway as rain-laden wind crashed past the stonework in vicious gusts. Janet said nothing for a long while, breathing heavily after the scramble back up the shore. "It'll be dark soon Bob, I want you to run down to the village, go out to Scarfhall and get Maggie to light a lamp in the east window, make sure it's turned up bright, two lamps if she can spare would be even better, if you can find an old looking glass set it behind the light. Go then down to the peedie pier at Gill and have your storm lantern lit, wave it high to guide us in".

"Guide you in… what the hell are you speaking about Janet"

"Don't you see Bob, yin ship can't survive out there much longer… once the ebb runs strong and the water shallows up it will be certain disaster. I must go and warn them. Come on Bob don't just stand there like an old blind sow, follow on and help me get faithers old dinghy down the beach."

"This is crazy Janet, you have no chance, the old boat is no big, it's maybe bonny painted again but you're just a peedie wife, you'll no survive one blink in this gale, out there beyond the point there is a real live storm, not a fireside story over a jug o' ale. How in the name of the Almighty do you think you can rescue a whole big ship wae a dinghy?"

"Don't argue Bob, what's more important; one undernourished spinster with nothing left in her life but a cripple dog to look after, or a dozen sailors wae bairns and families to support? I'm no sure I will succeed, however someone needs to do something and I'll be makin' tae help even if you don't."

It took them only twenty minutes to slip, trip and scramble their way along the shore of the Ouse, towards old Jocks dinghy lying in its noust on the north side of Skaill bay. Many coats of tar added extra weight to the old hull and the two of them struggled to get her moving towards the water despite having lifted out most of the movable parts. Short bursts of strenuous heaving got the dead weight moving over turf and stones and frequent stops were needed to gather strength and catch breath. Bob looked down towards the shoreline to where the tide was rising; "looks like the tide won't get much higher" he shouted into the wind, as they slid the boat with a final heave into the water. "Aye Bob, it'll be on the turn soon…no time to spare…."

"We're under the lee of the land right here Janet where things look no too bad, but think about it lass, out past the headland the full force of the wind will hit, it's no safe, the white water will be waiting oot bye…"

"Put more effort into your muscles than your tongue Bob and fetch me the oars".

"You are a dogged wife Janet, you'll surely die a hero".

Up to his knees Bob pushed the boat into deeper water and as the old dinghy began to float he grabbed the stern rope and held tight, Janet scrambled aboard and hoisted the fully reefed neckerchief-sized lugsail onto the mast and turned back to Bob. A gust caught the canvas and rolled the dinghy over on to her beam as Janet dropped the rudder onto the pintles, wrapping her arm around the tiller she shouted "Let go Bob, I'm off, this is it, no stopping now, make haste and go like the wind to the village".

"Oh God be with you Janet, tho'll need all the help thoo can get" Bob shouted as he waded back up the beach cold and very wet, wondering if he had told Janet his inner feelings whether it would have made any difference… "Naa she never got over Ben, he'll be with her in her last breath". Bob looked back over his shoulder and tried to imprint the image of the tiny sail in his memory as it disappeared into another rain squall. "Might never see you again lass, they'll blame me for letting you go…" Bob scrambled over the dunes and faced the fierce wind, filling his eyes with sand.

Janet hunkered down in the bilge and braced herself against the stern thaft, her eyes scrunched tightly, peering through salt laden spray, the northerly blast from behind drove the tiny dinghy on its one way journey….she could hear old Jock's words in her head:
"Thoo are a dogged lass Janet, like thee grandmither. When thoo pits thee mind tae hid nobody can stop thee, so mak sure thoo gets hid right first time…nobody gets a second bite o' the cake".

The bow of the dinghy dug deep into unseen waves as darkness descended. It became increasingly difficult to keep steering in a southerly direction as the frequent gusts took control of such a tiny cockleshell, rounding up into the wind and threatening to broach. The sail shook and spilled its contents as Janet struggled against the heavy tiller to bring the boat back on course. They were overpowered and something would have to give, probably sooner rather than later. Every wave seemed bigger than the last and reality began to dawn; there was a high possibility the end was very near. She found herself praying for the first time in her life..... "Oh God, I have never believed in you or any of what that awful minister tries to preach, however if you are really up there, now might be a good time to convert me... at least give me a fighting chance, right now.... please, please help....".

"What the..." Janet cried as a coil of old rope became dislodged from under the bow tulfer and floated back in the bilge water to her feet. "Thank you... thank you...." The heavy-duty rope was tied to a piece of chain and she hauled this back in desperation, threw it over the stern, ensuring one end was attached to the boat. It was long and heavy and had the immediate effect of slowing them down, keeping stern to wind and the boat more controlled. The inevitable broach had been averted, for a short while at least.

Water daggers pierced the back of Janet's head and stringy wet hair flailed sore across her face as she darted a screwed up glance behind to see rolling crests appear out of the darkness. Leaning her full weight over the tiller and with cold numb feet wedged against the timmers to get more purchase another wave broke over the stern and into the bilge. She tensed, waiting for the inevitable next and what must eventually be the fatal last wave to descend. Her eyes closed a couple of seconds as the

screaming wind eased and a grey shadow loomed ahead; the final abyss, a big hole leading directly into the earth's core had opened up, she figured this was the road many others before her had taken, she was not the first and certainly would not be the last. Death, Janet decided, might not be that bad at this moment, "just take me away, take me out of this great pain.... Ben will be waiting...."
The sail gave a mighty crack and a hundred pieces of canvas disappeared like confetti.

The trio on the beach were "beating flukes" as they watched over the anchored boat. "It's damned cold" Oliver o' Waal was saying, "but I'm sure it'll be worth the wait, when the tide turns she'll be ashore the night".
"Aye" responded Thomas "I don't ken what she carries but a cargo of rum would go down a treat right now" Holy mother.... look over yonder" he shouted to the others, "There's something out there.... a sail, there's no much daylight left but I think it's a green dinghy"

"Old Jock o Vere's skiff is green, it must have been swept off the shore wae all this wind" James o' Brough was saying as he jumped up on a higher ledge of rock and peered into the salty wind. Bloody boat has its sail up....done well to get this far...my God...look... the sail has blown, that'll be the end of a good fishing boat for sure".

Chapter VI

Bob stumbled and fell into a ditch as he ran across the field, it was getting darker and the horizontal rain made it difficult to see beyond a few feet. "Oh Janet" Bob said to himself as he ran with increasingly labored breathing, water squelched out his old worn leather boots every stride. "I should have stopped you I really should". Easing off to a slow walk as he came to the brow of the Brae o' Fiold he could make out a few lights in the village below between the showers. "No far to go now though." His chest was sore and pounding. Something moved in the field beside with a huge groan, a big wet nose met his own in the darkness as he leaped back from the stone wall and landed awkwardly. "Holy smoke...who got the biggest freight, me or you aald nag" Bob shouted. "Ease down, I mean no harm. Come here, stand apace, I could do with some help".

The pony wasn't very big but was placid and allowed him to mount. Holding tightly on to the long tangled main he dug in his knees to keep from slipping off. The pony took this as an order to trot and set off at a pace Bob was not prepared for, the fright in his voice was dulled by the sharp wind as he yelled "Slow boy slow, ease off for god's sake or I'll end up a bag o' broken bones". However, against all odds and despite becoming very pained Bob remained on the ponies back as they made their way through a deep mud track that had once been the village road.

The unlikely looking pair arrived at Scarfhall out on the headland across from Gill as the rain eased. Maggie was out in the dark battening up windows on the north side of her stone cottage with some drift wood. "Hi Maggie, don't worry it's only me" Bob shouted as he approached the gate.

Maggie hammered a wooden wedge into the makeshift shutter and glanced back over her shoulder. "Well I've seen it all noo...Bob on a horse, looking like he's been through the mill. Big blaw the night I doot Bob, I need to get me windows shuttered up afore they blow in". Maggie stopped and turned to face the bedraggled shape of Bob sliding off the pony. "Thoo all right, whit thoo dain' oot on a day like this? Thoo'r buxan', come in afore the fire, thoo'll catch thee death".

"I'm no' here to bide Maggie, can thoo spare a lamp for the ben window. There's a big boat coming up to anchor in the bay and they need a guiding light".

"No a night tae be oot there on the sea, poor beggars" Maggie said, "Whitever thoo needs Bob just taak. Thoo'll find twa lamps through ben". Bob lit the lamps and set them in the window, ensuring the rags Maggie had as curtains were removed and well clear of the flame. He made his way back to the door and thanked his old aunt for her help, "slok the lamps once thoo sees the boat safe at anchor Maggie. I must awa"

"Hoo's thee mither the day Bob, I heard she's no weel?"

"Sorry Maggie I don't have time tae yarn, must get doon tae Gill. She's a bit better the day though. Thanks for aaskan. I'll let thee ken how we get on".

Captain Mac was mighty glad to have found shelter; the run from Shetland to Liverpool was normally straight forward, however this early season gale blowing from the north had caught them unprepared as they passed Orkney, the notorious Boar of Papa Westray had been unavoidable. "Not a good place to be even on a bonny night" the local fishermen would say. Strong tides mixed with an opposing gale force northerly wind could develop into mountainous and unpredictable seas, whirlpools of legendary proportions were not uncommon in the Bore and many ships had been lost in this area over the years.
The Emily Jane was a large cargo boat, however had been laid on her beam ends in the center of the Bore like a paper toy in the mill burn, sails reduced to rags and a couple of lower yards torn from the mast. They had fought for hours until the tide turned and mercifully released them. "Sails and spars can be replaced" he was telling the Mate, "damned lucky to get out with most of the boat intact, let alone our lives."

"Aye captain", the mate agreed, "However this gale is still raging and the ship veering awkwardly on her anchor will make for a long night on watch"
"It was indeed good fortune to have escaped the Bore with our skins intact" said captain Mac, "however, like you, I'm a deep sea sailor and the sight of land scares me, never speaking of laying moored here so near the shore…"

Having limped their way through huge seas after such a traumatic knockdown the southerly passage down the sound between Papa Westray and Westray was the only option open left open; they no longer had enough sail power to make safe passage along the north of the Orkney islands.

Captain Mac looked across to the mate "More good luck than good guidance we found this anchorage, I have never been in among the Orkney islands before and reputation has it they are extremely challenging with strong tides not to be taken for granted.... darkness is closing in and the wind has eased none, I'm thinking we are particularly lucky to be moored up where we are."

"We all need some rest and tomorrow will bring its own worries when we have to prepare again for sea. Once you've tied up the worst of that flailing rigging, hoist up the anchor light and double-up lookouts on anchor watch rota, this gale is not over yet and the last thing we need is a dragging anchor. Ensure all crew doss down in the saloon so they can be roused at a couple of seconds notice should we need. If there is the slightest inkling the anchor might be dragging shout for all hands on deck; I recon we have a few miles clear to leeward, however with no charts I don't want to move more than a couple of yards".

Two sailors hunkered under the gunwale for'ard, glancing over the top every time the wind drew breath and before driving rain could soak them further, "these oilskins are bloody useless Tam, water goes straight down to me arse every time I look ower the rail".
"Ach haud yer wheesht min and keep an eye on the transits, I know it isn't easy to see in the darkness, however if we drag anchor in this wind it'll no be many minutes until we hit something hard to leeward and it'll be more than your arse that will get wet then".

"I canna see further than the end o' me nose....hang on...d'yu see that Tam?", Jim shouted "there's something out there, see way up to windward, brown shape, might be a sail..."
Tam looked over the rail...bloody hell... looks like a boat out there, a small sail indeed...maybe a dinghy and its coming this way fast...".

After the sail blew out Janet wrapped the trailing rope around the tiller and crawled forward on her knees, waist deep in water she wrapped her arms around the mast. The situation was grim and the end was probably very near. She could sense her beloved Ben looking down from somewhere far above. "Help me Benjamin, I'm so scared, but I have changed my mind, I came out here to help others, I'm not ready to join you yet" she shouted into the wind as another gust bowled the dinghy over. The boat was now wallowing lower as every wave seemed to pass through rather than under the tiny hull.

Jim ran aft shouting to alert the crew as Tam made a lunge into the locker and hauled out a rope together with a large monkey's fist and tied it to the end of the light heaving line. Coiling it into large loops he shouted across to the men arriving on the foredeck pulling on jackets. "It's getting here fast and I think there might be someone on board....only one chance lads, only one chance...I'm going to throw the line like it's on the life of me first-born. If it doesn't work yon dinghy will be past wir stern in twa blinks and will never be seen again.

Tam braced himself against the rail while one of the other crewmen clung to the rigging, he twisted his cap peak around to the back and grimaced into the wind driven rain. "Here it comes, Tam, bide your time, not too soon.....wait...I'll hold on to your belt so's you can lean as far out over the rail as possible... let him have it Tam, heave it out, I hope he manages to catch the rope".

The line coiled out over the bow quarter and rose against the wind, the heavy rope ball appeared to stall for a couple of heart stopping moments before being whipped out of midair by a sudden lull and dropped like a stone towards the now very low riding boat. Tams yells of delight were drowned as the wind gusted again and tore the words from his lips.

Janet caught sight of some movement high above "Oh my god, it's the ship" the huge black hull was there, dead ahead... a tangled lump of rope seemed to hover high over the bow for a second and fell into the dinghy, she lunged forwards, grabbed and wrapped it around the mast in one determined and final action.

"Throw the boarding net over the side...now" captain Mac shouted as he grabbed the end of the heaving line and tied it to a cleat.

The tiny boat halted its manic journey across the waves and healed over dangerously, turning a hundred and eighty degrees as the rope came fast and was swept against the side of the ship in a mast-splintering crash. Captain Mac slung a rope around his waist and clambered down the boarding net, "hold on to this Tam, I'm going down for yon poor man, don't let go...Holy mother of god... It's a wife" he shouted up as he descended into the melee ..."a bloody wife" he called back up to Tam as his cold white fingers grasped tightly on to the netting.

Chapter VII

Janet opened her eyes and peered over a grey itchy blanket, she could see her jacket hanging over the back of a small mahogany chair, dripping water onto the wooden floor. The flickering light of a small oil lamp reflected in a mirror as it swung back and forth. Shivering with cold she sat upright and tried to take in the surroundings, "I'm alive" she shouted through chattering teeth "how long have I been in here....what time is it?"

"Ah my dear girl, you have plenty volume, I guess you're going to make it. It's half past the hour of five." said captain Mac as he peered around the door and stepped into the cabin dropping the pocket watch back into his waistcoat pocket. "What in hells name were you doing out there in that small boat, you'd have been a goner for sure if we hadn't been in your way and picked you out of that crate. What possessed you to venture out on a day like this?"

"You, that's what possessed me, I'm here because of you. Your ship is in danger. Are you the captain? Believe me, you must move and move now, the tide will be turning in a short while and by the sound of it the wind must still be forty knots if it's a whisper. With an ebb tide running north at over six knots as it does here in Papay Sound I can guarantee your boat will not survive the night.... The conditions will create a reception like the Devil himself could not put on at the gates of Hell should you be unfortunate enough to be invited"

"All right lassie, I understand, I know the tides are strong in these Islands, however we are in a fine sheltered spot here and will be moving on in the morning when the wind will surely ease. I would not ordinarily venture somewhere like this without charts or pilot, however we survived the Bore off the north of Papay and needs must....luckily we arrived here in one piece to lick our wounds.
If the wind does not ease shortly I may have to deploy another anchor and wait until the good Lord decides it is time for us to move".

Janet leapt from the bunk, her legs so weak she staggered and almost collapsed, captain Mac grabbed her and sat her down on the chair. "Ride out the storm here? That is not an option, believe me sir, captain, mister, whatever...you need to move. I have lived along these shores all my life and know you will not be able to stay here, no matter how many anchors you have. The bay around at Waal is the only bay in this area that can provide some shelter in a northerly gale. Please believe me...you must move and move now before it's too late".

"It's black dark out there lassie, no sight of a moon, we can't see a thing, I don't know where this safe haven lies, even if we did it would be madness to move without a chart or pilot".

"It will be madness not to move Captain, Captain...what's your name did you say?"

"Sorry Janet, excuse my manners, Mac is my name, Captain John Mac."

"I cannot stress enough Captain Mac, it is full scale suicide to do nothing. I've already organized lights to guide us into the bay and I assume you have a compass. I would ken me way round these shores wae me eyes poked out, I will guide you around to the sheltered bay, I will be your pilot. Do not underestimate the gravity of your situation captain and do not underestimate me either, I might only be a lass to you but have more wit and wile than your average old salty tar, believe me I have a determination that will not let any of you perish. I came out here to help and help I bloody will. Any way…how do you ken I'm called Janet?"

You were ranting and raving as we carried you to the cabin, introducing yourself as Janet Forsyth and demanding to see someone called Benjamin Garrioch….

"Oh…sorry…I will explain later…We are wasting precious time captain, please believe and trust me we must move and move now before the ebb tide takes hold."

Captain Mac disappeared through the doorway. "Everyone on deck, get your oilies on we're on the move, get ready to hoist what's left of the headsails"

Leaning back into the cabin he said "Janet you are a persuasive wife, I don't know why but I'm trusting you, I hope I'm doing the right thing…my god I so hope you know what you are doing. We'll be under your control in five minutes flat, grab your coat and meet me on deck…."

The winter afternoon was already black dark and a cold wind pierced through her damp clothing as Janet stood in the lee of an unlit binnacle, holding tight against icy blasts she closed her eyes to help gain some night sight. Holding her hand to sheild her eyes she opened them again and could just make out the compass card pointing due north.

Captain Mac barked a few orders to the mate as he stumbled forward holding on to the rail. "We are veering around with this wind like a rum-filled tar; as soon as the headsail catches the wind we will begin to turn, make sure the anchor is winched up rapidly as it trips".

Three times they crept towards and across the wind with the headsail vibrating, the anchor rope pulled tight but did not release. "She's not going to come through the wind captain, the anchor has come fast".

"OK we can't hang on any longer, cut the cable as soon as she catches the next gust, we need to get out of here now." bellowed captain Mac. "Untie the Starboard anchor and get her ready to use, take a couple of hands and move the spare kedge up from aft and make it ready to deploy on the opposite rail."

Two swipes of the axe released them from the seabed. The big hull turned, slowly at first, then, as both headsails filled she leaned to starboard and swept her wide stern across the dark north sky. The whole ship became quieter as they picked up speed, rolling in slow motion before the wind. "Can you see anything Janet? I can't make out a bloody thing beyond the bowsprit."

"The moon seems to be well hidden by all this cloud cover indeed, but don't worry Captain, I can see enough between the showers to ken where we are, keep her steady on this course, it looks good."

"Steer South South West Mr. Stokes, we don't want her getting blown too far east. I see a glimmer of light low down to the west Janet, is that anything to do wae you?".

"Probably yon murderous wreckers camped out on the beach waiting for your demise. This course looks good captain, we are in deep water here, however not very far from the shore, we need to be ready to turn in about a mile and a half".

"That's only a few blinks away with all this wind up our stern." Captain Mac shouted across, "Don't let her over run your turning point mind, we'll never claw back to windward with these small headsails if we don't get this right." He turned his back to the wind and made a silent prayer…

As they progressed south the darkness was all encompassing and Captain Mac strode back and forth across the after deck, his heavy jacket collar wrapped up tight around his ears. "Steady on the helm there, if that flames are on the shore, we don't want her drifting any nearer, it's probably only a cable or so away mind and those rocks are mighty hard…."

The rigging howled again as another gust arrived with a shower of rain, the big masts remained doggedly steady running before the wind into the darkness ahead. Captain Mac had to confess to himself as they were swept along that this could be the worst and possibly the last decision of his career.

Janet had no definite plan when she set off in the dinghy other than to organise the guiding light and to warn the sailors of their danger, assuming they would have a chart and make haste to a better anchorage, however here she was standing alongside the captain, in control, calling the shots. She had never been in charge of anything bigger than a Westray skiff and had never been on board a boat this size before. She was scared, her fingers were white and numb with holding on to the binnacle rail. Her inner self however was strangely calm and she knew what was required, she knew what to do and was making it happen.

As the wind obscured any conversation, Janet found herself openly speaking to Ben, she was asking him to help guide them in and keep them safe.
The rain really needed to stay away until it was possible to pick up the light in Scarfhall, which should be only a couple more minutes or so to the west after they cleared the point of Berridale. Headsail sheets were led around the winches with only a couple of turns and no hitches on the cleats, in readiness to release at the drop of a hat. Braced against the moving deck a bedraggled crew scoured the distant darkness for signs of danger, waiting for their captain to give orders.
These men were fully aware their lives were now in the hands of someone who had never mastered a ship before which was bad enough, but this someone was a woman. An early grave was more than likely to be the outcome of such foolhardiness, however they had been persuaded by their captain that the option to stay was even more likely to end in disaster. They were a devoted and able team who had sailed together for many years and shared the greatest respect and admiration for Captain Mac, despite this their cooperation was given with some trepidation.

Minutes passed without any words being uttered, the occasional flash of captain Mac's eyes revealed nothing as he waited for this tiny figure to dictate the next move. Janet could sense rather than see the headland, and she waited…. and waited…. The reality of what she was doing made her legs feel weak again.

The captain had ensured she knew the consequence of running too far south and the fact he had said it numerous times since they were underway did not help her nerves. One wrong call at this stage would spell the end and if they did indeed mistime the turn into the bay they would be swept south towards the skerry at Skelwick or beyond to the island of Eday, where storm tossed seas combined with the ebb tide, would mean a certain end.

"Turn, turn to starboard… turn now" Janet suddenly shouted, "I can see the light and the hill outlined above, I see it down low on the shore…we are clear of the point… turn…. now."

Captain Mac was in no position to doubt and did not hesitate, his ships safety now firmly in the hands of this firey woman, he jumped across and grasped the spokes of the large wooden wheel together with the helmsman and as one they turned her on to a west south west course towards the low flickering light in the distance. Windage aloft became a scream as the ship swung around and heeled over dramatically on her larboard beam. Captain Mac barked an order for the crew to take up slack in the sails as they flailed, the boat was on a beam reach with only two headsails to power them onward.

"Make ready the anchors, ensure they are both free and have blades ready to cut the lashings as soon as I give the order… we'll set them both, I'll give the order to drop the Starboard anchor first, then, on the count of twenty release the second, no room to get it wrong as well you know."

Janet stood on the lee rail, arms wrapped around the aft mast rigging pointing ahead, "Do you still see the light Captain, down low under the bow? I think we need to be a bit further north…"

"Bring us a few points further up to Starboard" Captain Mac shouted to the helm, "don't let her fall down to leeward…aye, fine there, hold her steady at that."

The guiding glimmer of yellow light increased in size as they sailed Janet's course under staysail, only having seamlessly dropped the jib to create a more controlled approach.

"Oh Hell Janet I hope you know what you are doing" captain Mac said as the light in Scarfhall window guided them nearer to the anchorage, "If I say I'm scared it's no exaggeration, my breex will be ready for dumping after this".

"Keep that peedie light ahead where it is over the bow captain, we are doing well along here with the shore only half a cable on the weather side, there's not much depth along this shoreline and very little room once we get closer to the shallow point off Scarfhall which runs a good way up from the south. Keep the sail full and maintain our speed as we approach, don't let her drift any more to leeward. I'm guessing we need every inch of momentum we can muster to make the turn, maybe we should have kept that other sail up as well…"

"Don't worry Janet, you just show me where to go and I'll show you how to do it…"

"I'm looking out for someone waving a light on the jetty below Gill to the north, we will be very near the rocks at that stage, as soon as I call out you need to turn ninety degrees to Starboard."

"I'll drop the sail immediately we turn as it might backfill and throw her head across the wind," captain Mac explained, "the weight of the ship will ensure we keep moving ahead for a few boat lengths once we are bow up to the wind, the very second she loses forward momentum I will shout for the anchors to drop."

Janet was beginning to shake with cold and her initial adrenalin burst was fading, "Oh captain, I hope this is going to work… I'm beginning to lose confidence, I so hope this is going to work…" Janet confessed aloud as she watched captain Mac wipe the salt spray dripping down his face.

"Hell lass, keep your eyes on the marks, too late to get your brain in a mix now…so far so good. The wind is getting less as we approach under the lee of the land, I feel things are a bit more under control again. You tell me when to turn and get us round this bit without ripping out the keel and I'll dance at your wedding".

"It's them, bloody hell it's them" shouted Bob as he stood in the lee of the storehouse, "I can see a light high up in the rigging, fast approaching". The clouds parted long enough for an outline of the large dark hull to be seen heading towards the point of Scarfhall. "The lamp Johnny, grab the lamp fast, we need to be out on the jetty to guide them in right now." Bob had his brother helping with the storm lantern and together bowed their heads to the wind and supported each other along the slimy seaweed surface of the stone jetty. Bob shouted pointlessly across the wind and water as he swung the lamp above his head "Over here Janet, over here, turn now you crazy bitch, you're clear of the point."

Chapter VIII

Wall bay was bathed in yellow-pink as an early morning sun rose from the south east., the still waters seemed eerily quiet following two days of constant howling gales. Emily Jane swung easily on two limp anchor cables, her rigging creaked a little, dripping heavy dewdrops onto the deck. Captain Mac rose cold and damp from his nest of coiled up ropes in a corner of the pushpit having finally fallen asleep during his shared all night anchor watch. He had not dared venture down to the cabin as Janet had been sent there once they had safely settled to anchor.

"A strong hot brew and eggs for breakfast would be in order for all the crew Mr Cook" he suggested to the figure appearing up the companionway.
"Oh sorry Janet I thought it was the cook appearing up for his morning smoke. You're early, didn't expect to see you for another couple of hours at least."

"Captain, I think I should go ashore, the island tongues will already be wagging I have no doubt. Have you got a seaworthy dinghy left."

"Aye as soon as you wish lass, I'll get some breakfast underway first, assuming there might be a whole egg left on board, we are all a bit famished.
First though a confession; that storm was tough, probably one of the worst of my career, I do not want to have to endure anything like that again. I am the first to admit to have been totally unprepared for the situation we found ourselves in and believe I might just be getting too old for this way of life. The Bore off the north o' Papa Westray

should have been avoided, then running into Orkney waters with no charts and no end plan was not a balanced decision. We very nearly lost the ship and more importantly, the lives of my crew. And to top this whole ordeal we must come to terms with the fact that a woman…."

"Stop right there Captain Mac, I am Janet Forsyth, a barren spinster living on a one sheep croft on the island of Westray, my parents are dead, my fiancé was lost at sea, I have no money, the locals think I am a witch….yes, just a useless, weak and down-trodden woman to many perhaps, but do not underestimate what you might call the weaker sex Captain. There is more inside this woman's heed than a dozen men put together, call me down as an individual if you want, I know I'm not perfect, but do not generalize the female species, believe me, the weaker sex will be your equal one day and when that day comes….."

"Wow, stop, bloody hell…. I am speechless.
Sorry, really I am, I didn't mean it that way. I promise I am not your average male bully… I seldom underestimate the abilities of the fairer sex. I can assure you, with four daughters still living at home I have learned to respect and value the wisdom of a woman's word.
Your selfless actions and huge natural ability demonstrated yesterday Janet, has reinforced my respect. My boat was facing certain disaster and fearlessly you stepped in to help. Janet, you are a brave, selfless, very smart and extremely able woman, I do not know another person, male or female, who could have firstly, convinced me to move from my anchorage and secondly, could have piloted my ship to safety in such extreme conditions. I am truly humbled and intend to let everyone know what you

did, I have no doubt my agents will come with a handsome thank you".

"Sorry captain, forgive me, I didn't mean to come with such an outburst, I really do not mean to offend, I know you are a good person. I am pretty mixed up at the moment and I do not have anyone to vent off my frustrations to anymore", She touched his sleeve and looked him in the eye, "I do not need your agent's gifts, what I did was for you, your crew and their families.
You might want to direct thanks to that gang of wreckers waiting on the beach last night, it was them who drove me into frenzied action...mercenary get rich quick wreakers, they would have let you die on the shore while plundering the spoils of your storm battered cargo.
I had nothing when I entered this world, I need nothing when I leave, should your agents wish to part with money then a contribution to the Poor House in Kirkwall would be appreciated."

Janet jumped onto the gunwale and pointed towards the shore. "Here comes the flit boat, helmed by no other than that two-faced rat Michael Balfour from Noltland. He'll be all smiles and full of promises, however keep your eye on him Captain, he'll have the shirt off your back before you leave port if he possibly can. Put a guard on watch as long as you are anchored here and have repairs done in Kirkwall. I know you have no charts, however I drew a rough pilot sketch and left it on your cabin table; go south on the flood tide and anchor up in Deer Sound, you will save a berthing and pilot fee and the excise man won't bother you there. Ask for Peace's sailmakers; married to my cousin Bess, John is a fair man and will give you a good price to sort your canvas"

You're one crazy woman Janet Forsyth" said Michael Balfour as he stepped aboard the Emily Jane, I saw you out in the teeth of that gale; you're bloody lucky this ship caught you before you disappeared over the horizon and met your watery grave. What the hell were you doing out there in that small dinghy?"

"I do not seem to have had the pleasure…" Captain Mac stepped forward looking for a handshake. "My name is John Mac captain of this ship…….."

"Forgive me Captain, I am Michael Balfour, Laird of most of the west side of this island. I come to wish you well and to offer my assistance."

"I can only assume Mr Balfour you have not been informed as to how we came to be anchored in the heart of your beautiful island community?"

"Ah indeed captain, I observed your misfortune yesterday from the shore, I am so glad you were able to realise the danger you were in and make safe passage into Wall Bay before you were driven onto to that rocky shore, as surely would have happened in the conditions we experienced last evening. I can see you have suffered some damage aloft that might delay your onward passage and hope I might be of service to you in that respect, I have some very good carpenters and sail makers in my employ".

"Thank you good sir for your offer of help, however I see you might benefit from an update on your knowledge; Putting her own life in peril, Janet here set sail in a tiny boat to warn us of the great danger into which my ship had been placed, her knowledge of these waters is sound and her ability to pilot a ship in the conditions we encountered yesterday is likened to someone who has spent a lifetime at sea, the proof of which is in our presence here today. In short Mr Balfour, she saved our lives."

The hunched shoulders of Michael Balfour twitched nervously as he stood, looking through Janet as she glared back in defiance. He made no effort to respond to captain Mac's words.

"I intend to make haste while the weather holds" offered Captain Mac in the silence of the moment, "we will depart on the early flood tomorrow morning. Can I offer you a glass of fine port Mr Balfour, in the comfort of my cabin before we breakfast?"

His ice blue eyes darted across to captain Mac but rested again on Janet's defiant glare. "Thank you no, captain, I do not think you should waste precious time on entertainment, I see there is a week's work aloft to complete before your morning tide". Turning again to Janet, his face grey and unfriendly; "Can I offer our storm hero a lift ashore Miss Forsyth? You might want to use the time in my boat to expand on how you gained these wonderous skills".

Captain Mac stepped in before Janet could respond, "Thank you again for the offer of help Mr Balfour, please excuse us a moment".
He took Janet's arm and walked her to the rail, "I can see what you mean Janet, I do not trust that man, he is not to

be trusted,", he said in a hushed voice. "Come with us to Kirkwall in the morning, there is nothing left for you in this island, I know I could find you gainful employment without any problem, with your many talents you would fare well in the busy south"

"Thank you Captain" Janet's head bowed as a tear rolled down her cheek, his firm grip was reassuring, looking into his eyes she saw the warm compassion of a man who resembled her father in many ways. "You are a kind person and your offer I know is genuine, and very tempting. I have dreamed of taking that step captain, many times but too have too many loose ends to tidy up and some soul searching to do, I cannot just up sticks quite yet. I will consider your offer very seriously though."

"Miss Forsyth", Mr Balfour barked in her direction as he strode towards the gunwale, "I am departing and suggest you accept, unless you want your reputation on this island to plummet another few degrees, another night aboard this ship may however be how you wish to continue…"

Janet looked into the eyes of one of the few people left she really trusted, "I believe this episode may have sewn the seed of change captain, thank you for helping me believe in myself, I think I may not be far from that big decision after all."

"Goodbye Janet, your actions will not go unrewarded, do not wait too long to make that move and look me up when you get settled. Hold on a minute while I get something from my cabin".

Captain Mac reappeared with a small canvas bag and shoved it into Janet's hands, "It is nothing much lass, but just a small thank you from us all. I look forward to seeing you soon again."

The rumble of leather clad wooden oars broke the morning silence across Wall bay. Michael Balfour had been staring at Janet as the two oarsmen watched them both in silence, dipping oars in and out of the still water, never uttering a word. The small boat slid gently on to the sandy beach and grabbing her arm he stopped her before she stepped into the shallow water; "So, what's all this hero worship, saving lives shit? You must have been keeping the old captain warm in his cabin last night to have such praise heaped upon someone he met barely twelve hours ago".

"Your mouth Mr. Balfour as usual, appears to be contaminated with a very disagreeable virus, I hope it doesn't spread to your brain as that piece of rotting meat will not survive much more damage." Janet quipped, striding over the side onto the beach, her britches became rapidly soaked as she sloshed, shoulders held firm, through the water. "I had intended to thank you for the lift ashore" she shouted over the heads of the sniggering oarsmen, "however it is your poor slaves here that put in all the effort and seldom get thanks….so thank you both and my sympathy follows. Good day Mr. Balfour."

Bob stood waiting on the beach with Salty straining to the limit on a piece of string
"Hi Salty old boy, at least you are pleased to see me". She said with a heavy sigh "Oh Bob what a night, thanks for coming down. That Laird is a dangerous bastard, no

64

question. Will you walk me home? I am tired and I might need a bit of support". They tramped the guttery road towards Vere with Bob asking question after question.

"Thanks for everything Bob, especially for last night, I wouldn't have been able to manage without the light. You are always such a support, especially since Ben..... However I really need to lie down a couple of hours..." her walking became labored and she was beginning to feel a bit disorientated as they approached the house, "will you be a dear and see if there are any eggs down by the joiner shed, I might need something to eat later". She undid the tangled rope door latch and disappeared inside.

Chapter X

A blustery cold wind flogged the sails in anger as a shower passed overhead throwing wooden egg boxes around the old ferryboats hold. The Westray Firth was in its usual angry state Janet thought as a strong ebb tide pushed against the north westerly wind, she tried to move away from the revolting bundle of sheep skins under her head, however with hands tied behind her back it was impossible to sit and she let go a huge sigh. "Aha the witch has come to life" a voice boomed, "no point in struggling you'll just make it worse" the crewman said as he looked her over for a couple of minutes. Janet lay on her side squinting over the stinking pillow at the man as he filled his pipe with tobacco. Putting his head on one side and then the other as though trying to piece her together, the crewman lowered his voice and asked "Does thoo need some water?"

"Aye" Janet responded suspiciously, keeping eye contact.

The crewman returned with a flask and held it to her mouth as he lifted her head "I guess there is a bonny face under all that muck".

"Don't even think about it" she retorted as she spat out a mouthful of water.

"Don't worry lass" he said, "I'm just trying tae help, I'll no hurt thee, It's yin big red headed laird that deserves thee anger, seems he's been lukin' for an excuse to hiv thee arrested for a long while noo?" The crewman helped her drink some more and laid her head back on the hard wooden floor boards. "Thoo better keep quiet and lay still,

I've met yin lawman sat out in there in the stern, he's no the type thoo wants tae cross, I'll sit here until we get tae Kirkwall and he'll no bother thee".

Janet closed her eyes again and tried to recall events leading up to this point. The latter part of last night was a bit vague, probably something to do with the bleeding headwound. It had been a cold dark evening and she had gone to bed early after cleaning out the water barrel and taking in some firewood. Propped up on her freshly stuffed hay bolster looking into the canvas bag captain Mac had given her, with a cup of warm milk stood on the shelf at the back of the box bed.
"Oh my God" Janet cried...."money" She had counted three pounds in shillings, with more in the bag when the door flew open blowing out the candle. A loud crash of splintering table introduced several men into the dark cottage, shouting and cursing. Hands were all over her body dragging her out of bed, she bit calloused fingers as they tried to shut her screaming up; "Dirty bastards, get off me or you will suffer", she made a grab for a knife at the back of the box bed.

Salty was barking, there was a great deal of swearing and confusion when Janet heard a voice she recognized from her morning encounter, "Shut the witch up, get a light over here and tie her bloody hands".
"The whore has cut me Sir." was the last thing Janet recalled before waking up amongst ferry cargo in the early morning.

The ferry boat docked alongside the corn slip on the harbor front, Janet's hands had been re-tied in front to lead her up the slipway and bundled unceremoniously into a waiting carriage. One very short and smelly law officer sat beside her with a leather chord attached to the wrist ties. Sitting up and looking out between the bars of the black coach she could see a number of drunken men stagger out from one of the shore street bars. "The Westray boat is in boys, let's go and see what's come in fae north o' the Galt."

They caught site of the sheriff carriage and predictably homed in like sharks to a spill of blood. "Awe bless my soul, what have we here then my old porter guzzlers? A pretty maid all made up for a night out with the sailor boys" the first staggering wit to arrive called out. "You don't seem to have put much effort into making yourself pretty for the boys tonight" he squeaked, "and I'll wager a guinea to a farthing you'll no longer be a maid if you spent the day aboard the ferry with officer Dunn here beside you."
A dozen other drunken souls appeared and were arranging themselves in a gaggle around the carriage, "Give's a look boys, I can tell from a hundred yards if she's won Alfie his guinea". Seamus pushed in past the others and grabbed the carriage door bars "Well bless my soul boys, if it isn't Miss Janet Forsyth, I believe you will no be making a fortune betting on this one Alfie, she lost her maidenhood many years ago"

"And how wad thoo ken that now Seamus" asked the drunken rabble.

"I was working out in Westray the summer before last and all the island folk said she was looking for a man...so I obliged, many a night....door was always open".

"Like hell dirty lying waster, women are weel safe when thoo are around", Janet shouted back with tears running down her cheeks, "Saemus the shrew the Rousay women called thee… gossip travels fast Seamus, the Skello lasses held thee doon wan night and had a look…still no found anything I believe…." Seamus opened his mouth in retaliation, however the laughter drowned his words as the horse whip cracked and jolted the carriage on its way along the shore road.

Winding up through narrow cobbled streets the carriage rumbled noisily, hard iron clad wheels jolted the unsprung wooden transport box in all directions, throwing Janet and her escort around the inside like the last two peas in a jar. Janet could tell they were nearing the center of town as the stench grew worse. She recalled her first encounter with raw town sewage as a child; it wasn't just the overpowering smell and associated depravity, the final straw was the sight of seagulls pick at remains of a dead cat, making her physically sick and no one seemed to care. Returning home to the cold cottage on windswept Westray was heaven for an eight year old bairn after that experience.

The short lawman she now knew as officer Dunn led her unceremoniously through a series of dark passage ways into an unlit stone walled cell, the jailer laughed as she tripped and fell onto the urine stinking floor. A heavy silence fell once the echo of closing doors and keys ceased, the cold dark room wrapped itself around her hunkered figure in the corner. Janet was numb with cold and found she was too scared to cry.

Chapter XI

Sheriff MacDonald called for silence from the large crowd, his wooden gavel struck the lectern twice and a hush descended over the west wing of the Cathedral.

"The whole of bloody Kirkwall must be in here the day John Setter nudged his neighbor Thomas in the ribs as they jostled for a good view of the proceedings.

"Aye, nothing like the trial of a witch to draw out a crowd John boy, wish I had a penny for everyone here the day, that would pay for a week in town drinking the finest porter".
"Never mind, I got a fine price for the sheep skins this morning so I think a jar or two of ale to celebrate the witch's demise before we head home will be fine.

"Silence in the chamber" the sheriff called "Anyone found in breach will be tried with the witch and used as kindling".

A huge roar of laughter engulfed the crowd before a hushed expectant silence fell.
A door creaked open in the far corner and rain could be heard in the hush, rattling on the roof slates fifty foot above.
Janet was led across the chamber by a light rope tied to her hands. Torn and dirty clothing hung from her drooping shoulders as she walked behind the short stature of officer Dunn, his head held high and full of importance. Her figure standing in the prisoner dock, facing the jeering crowd was a pitiful sight.

"Order, order, the Court is now in session". The Sheriff held his right hand above his head like a preacher.

"In this year of our Lord, sixteen hundred and twenty nine, and on this day, the twenty seventh day of September, I hold court as required by the laws of our land to hear evidence of a particularly concerning nature.

The person we see presented here today is accused of a series of heinous practices and activity over a number of years.

She, ladies and gentlemen of our community, is accused of witchcraft……. a revultion in our midst that must be wiped out, a growth likened to the Black Death that cannot be permitted to contaminate the lives of decent people".

A cheer rose from the mesmerized crowd.

He continued; "Are you Janet Forsyth, residing at Vere, in the Island Parish of Westray?

Janet's head remained bowed and gave no answer.

"I will ask you again, be warned, should you choose not to answer you will be tried for contempt…believe me, you do not want that added to….I mean, you do not want that to contaminate my judgment of the accusations."

"Are you Janet Forsyth, living at the croft known as Vere, on the island of Westray?"

"Aye" Janet said without lifting her head.

"You are charged on two accounts:
One - with the crime of practicing witchcraft.

Two - resisting arrest to the serious injury of an officer of the crown."
How do you plead?"

Janet raised her head, "Oh my God man, this is rediculus, I am not a witch, there is no such thing….witchcraft is a term invented by religious fanatics for their own selfish ends….and none more so than your Reverend Hutton in Westray…a dangerous man Sheriff".

"I will ask you once again, Miss Forsyth, please do not launch into your defence speech at this point, you will be given time enough to defend the accusations." The Sheriff raised his voice, "How do you plead?"

Janet looked across the silent front row of witnesses, all known to her. Moving her head slowly right and left her words were edged with steel "Not Guilty."
She paused, looking up into the never ending ceiling of the vast cathedral and drew a deep breath;
"This is just plain ignorance, if I was a witch do you really think I would have let things get this far? Do you think that if I was a witch I would not have put a spell a long time ago on these self-centered, greedy, malicious individuals you have brought in to testify against me?
Listen to reason, witchcraft does not exist. The word is a malicious label attached to women of intelligence by those who are inherently stupid and fear what they are unable to comprehend or understand."

The crowd were loving it, comments from the accused were rare and for someone to put their head so far above the parapet at this stage was fueling the outcome nicely. A buzz of excitement began to rise.

"Not guilty" Janet sat down, visably shaking, with her head in her hands. I cannot keep this up she thought. "your situation is not good, put a brave face on it" the Kirkwall minister advised this morning during his visit to her cell, however she had pointed out it was her duty to publically name his Westray colleague as a corrupt and dangerous man. She was not opposed to religion or its preachers, however she wouldn't be in this position if it had not been for that particular obsessive witch hunter.
If nothing other was to come out of this case of legal murder she hoped it could be that the Kirkwall minister would look into her accusations and that he may find she was not the first to be persecuted by Mr Hutton and would not be the last. The minister had promised to follow up her request.

However, a brave face, she reflected was not going to alter the outcome of this sham trial.

"We have several witnesses here today" Sheriff MacDonald advised the crowd, "who will stand before the sword of justice and give evidence in the name of Almighty God. On the island of Westray, Reverend Hutton has been instrumental in gathering evidence and we are blessed today to have island residents and devoted followers of truth and justice to support and present the case on his behalf."

Alexander Stewart took one pace forward, turned towards the crowd holding up the large white scroll to a shaft of daylight beaming through the east window and began to read: "We, the undersigned declare to have witnessed and observed the accused, Janet Forsyth, carry out practices and behavior akin to and in the following of, the ancient practice of Witchcraft"

A heavy silence had been hanging over the audience which was broken by a communal intake of breath as the words 'witchcraft' were read out.

In his monotonous droll, Alexander Stewart listed the names of those present who had also signed the scroll:

> *Alexander Stewart – Cleat.*
> *Michael Balfour – Garth/Noltland.*
> *James Craigie – Broch.*
> *John Berstan – Noup.*
> *Robert Monteith – Egilsay.*
>
> *Thomas Rendall,*
> *Thomas Rendall (elder),*
> *Oliver Howieson,*
>   *All of Rackwick,*
>
> *Oliver Donaldson.*
> *William Rendall.*
> *John Setter.*
> *Thomas Howieson.*
> *William Harcus.*
> *Boneface Leask.*
> *Robert Low.*
>   *All of Waal*

"There have been many, many incidents over a long lot of years, possibly her lifetime we suspect.....and we know many others who can bear witness, however are unable to be present today. We have been tasked to instance but only three today for the purpose of keeping this trial as short as possible."

"My first" Mr Stewart continued after clearing his throat "On the 8th day of May 1625 a gimmer was lambing in a field belonging to my honorable friend Hamish Peterson. The shepherd was assisting the birth of twins, however one was born dead and left for the scavenging blackbacks to devour. Miss Forsyth was seen on this occasion to be passing bye and with the aid of a shepherds stick and stones to be shooing the birds away from their meal. She cleared the stone wall in one leap and picked up the dead lamb and give it what can only be described, forgive me your honour, but she delivered a long and indecent kiss, swung it around her head and laid it on the grass. This she did three times. As sure as I stand here before God I swear the animal stood up and ran to its mother."

"Devils work for sure" came the whispers from the crowd"

Alexander Stewart continued, "There are many, many stories like this I could relate; she has taken animals back from the dead, she has frozen the very insides of perfectly healthy animals and she has cast spells on God fearing islanders who has crossed her path...."

"Mr Stewart, I told you three stories are all I need you to relate...we will be here all night if you start into your fireside yarns."
The crowd laughed nervously and hushed into a quiet as they awaited the second story.

"The second story is told by my good friend William Rendall" who is a farm servant at Waal ". You could hear a pin drop as Mr Rendall stepped up and stood beside the sheriff. His stature wasn't any more than officer Dunn's and with little to no hair on his pale head he looked quite timid with small darting eyes. His voice was low and Alexander Stewart shouted at him to speak up as had been practiced.

"Three years past this month my mother Maggie died. A poorly soul, bed-ridden in latter years with her lungs full of gunge. Every day during the final weeks on this good earth she had been coughing her insides up, and with no strength left in her on the Sunday night she asked me to fetch the lass from Vere; "She has a way with herbs and cures, get her here Wullie"...for that's my name..., "get her here as soon as thoo can.
Well I did and she was in my house, boiling up a pot of the most disgusting smelling stuff you could imagine, there was mint and clover, malt and vile smelling onions and God kens what else.
She put a cloth over mother's head and left her sitting beside the fire with the steaming pot of brew for over an hour.
The next day I declared a miracle had happened, mother was out of her bed, no more coughing and feeling more sprightly than she had in years. We were starting to wonder why we hadn't sought the services of this miracle worker sooner. Three mornings running mother was up cleaning the fire out before anyone else stirred. On the morning of the fourth day we found her laid out on the stone floor cold as iron, dead as a door nail. Her eyes, wide open, had fear in them I tell you, she had seen the Devil as sure as I stand here. That witches

> brew had taken her breath away in a most
> gruesome cruel and horrid way."

A deep mumbling rose from the crowd as they become visibly fuelled up by mention of the Devil. "Burn the witch" began a chant at the very back, one by one they all joined in until the drone resembled a religious chant. "Burn the Witch, burn the witch".

Sheriff MacDonald shouted over the heads of the mass who were pushing towards the front. "I declare anyone found in contempt of the laws of this land will be severely punished and that includes anyone in this building today who might be found to be troublesome. I warn you settle down or suffer the consequence alongside the accused".

"The final story we submit was witnessed by half the folk in the north end of Westray, not five days ago it was. I ask my friend James Craigie o' Broch to deliver the tale".

Mr Craigie stood tall handsome, he didn't need to stand upon the step to be seen, or heard. Tucking a hat under his arm he tweaked his moustache and darted a sideways glance at Janet as she stared his way. His slow dramatic demenor drew the attention of everyone in the building. Waiting for silence to reign he began to speak:

> "You all know about the northerly gale we had last
> week, blew every hen house and hay stack down it
> did that gale. Biggest blow we've had for at least
> four years past...
> A lot of folk were gathered on the beach under
> Vere watching this big ship come in to anchor
> under the lea. The sea was as bad as I've seen it out

> there between Papay and the Holmes, the wind and spray were horizontal and the day was as black as mithers Sunday best neepian".

A few nervous laughs were raised at this reference "I bid you Mr Craigie to keep to the point without trying to play the court jester."

James Craigie drew his eyebrows down and continued, looking straight into Janet's eyes.

> "A shout went up from one of the beach combers short before darkness fell, pointing to a small dinghy under sail approaching this large ship. It was being blown before the storm at great speed, the spray and spume made it difficult to see beyond your nose for most of the time, however between showers everyone there could identify the green hull belonging to old Jock Forsyth, or I should say his daughter Janet who is the last remaining Forsyth on the island. She was out there I tell you in the middle of that gale, on that peedie boat, all on her own. No one in their right mind would have removed a boat from it's noust that day without it being most certainly reduced to firewood. Well as sure as I stand here and witnessed by at least a dozen others she sailed that dinghy out and boarded that huge boat without mishap or worry.
> She apparently took command of the ship and piloted her into the safe anchorage of Wall Bay. No man I know could have survived that storm in a dinghy, never mind a spindly woman on her own.

She survived dammit, she survived where others surely would have perished. She openly fears no God, she doesn't even go to church on a Sunday......Nothing but witchcraft could have saved that ship that night, no-one but a witch could have survived that storm....."

The crowd remained eerily silent, James Craigie gave a short cough and handed the parchment to the sheriff.

Sheriff MacDonald read the final part out:
"I, Reverend Hutton, Christian preacher on the island parish of Westray endorse the above statements and have witnessed with my own eyes many more incidents that could support the accusation.
The signatures above are all authentic and witnessed by me without prejudice:"

Another throat clearing cough in the silence of the great building as the Sheriff handed the document back to Alexander Stewart.

The sheriff looked up and glared over the heads of the steaming crowd. "You have heard the evidence from Reverend Hutton, poor man was unable to present it himself today due to ill health, however you are able to appreciate its authenticity as it has been supported and signed by so many trustworthy members of the community.
He turned his head slowly towards Janet, who was staring in complete disbelief across at Alexander Stewart and the other 'stalwarts' of the Westray community.

Wiping the sweat from his brow the sheriff, for the first time looked a bit uneasy, a tick started in his left eye as he watched Janet for a few seconds. "Place your right hand on the Bible Mr Stewart. Do you swear that the evidence presented today is the whole truth and the statement in support by those listed is genuine... so help you God?

"Aye It is so. Oh and you might be interested to ken; she was counting out money the night she was arrested...ten pounds...now where would the bitch have come by that I ask you? She wouldn't tell us so you can figure that out for yourselves."

"That's enough Mr Stewart"
He then turned back to Janet, "You, Janet Forsyth did not only do these things by your witchcraft and delivery, but made it public that you had the skill to do these things which, rank witch, you cannot deny."

A low hiss arose from the crowd as the hazy steam rose from tightly packed bodies, they cheered, jeered and waved caps and bonnets at Janet who sat, shoulders slumped in the dock, defeated. The trial was completely one sided, with no remit to call a defence. Witch hunt was truly what it was and the crowd were after blood, she raised her head and looked through water filled eyes across the sea of waving arms. Four men in uniform had arrived through the main door and stood at the back watching events unfold, the fair haired one on the left removed his naval cap and wiped his brow.

Janet's heart stopped a brief moment as she rose to her feet gazing in disbelief across the huge cathedral hallway; she could see the tall handsome frame of Ben, her Ben. As their eyes locked he took a step forwards waving both hands in the air, his friends grabbed and held him back diverting him towards the door and away from this very unpredictable rabble.

"Ben, oh Ben, save me" she shouted across to where she had seen the four uniformed men "The world has gone crazy, I never needed you more than I need you now". She took one step out of the dock before two portly guards jumped to attention, grabbing her arms tightly. Janet stood on her tiptoes and scanned the back of the building, Ben was no longer there. "It was too good to be true, my eyes deceive me and my mind plays tricks." She sat down and openly wept.

"Orkney is a fair and good place to live," sheriff McDonald was preaching "let no man or woman upset the peace and tranquility of our glorious islands. Good will defeat evil in the name of our Lord and Saviour.
I hereby declare you Janet Forsyth to be guilty as charged.

A huge came from the crowd.

"Silence, silence before I choose someone to join the witch.......
A pyre will be constructed at Gallow Hill midday tomorrow where Janet Forsyth will be hanged until dead and the devil burned from the body. The remains to be scattered across unconsecrated ground on the St Ola boundry."

Take her now to Marwicks Hole and make sure you post your best guards" the sheriff shouted, "before this crowd take things into their own hands and deny us tomorrows pleasure."

Chapter XII

It was well into the evening when Janet awoke cold and damp in the cell. A small glimmer of light from the barred window outlined a dented tin mug and the untouched bread roll from her morning meal, she took a sip of water but spat out something floating on top "Oh Hell and Damnation" she yelled and slumped back on the bench. "This is probably as low as things can possibly get; a witch, how the hell do they think I could be a witch. I should have moved away from this wretched land when I first got the chance, I would have found my fortune in the land of milk and honey by now…or maybe I would have fared no better, I'll never know now." An echoing silence fell as she recalled past years; the good bits when she was growing up and life was eternal sunshine, the bad bits when death had visited these latter years, everyone she ever loved was now gone, I hope someone is looking after Salty. Bob has been a good friend, I owe him so much, I never managed to say goodbye but hope he will understand; He'll have picked up the old dog…at least the dog will miss me…probably Bob will also….
She couldn't forget the vision of Alexander Stewarts bowed bald head as she was led towards Marwick's Hole, past the group of Westray stalwarts, he didn't have the nerve to look up as she slowly passed. His smooth dome was white and shiny as though the sun had never risen over the big house of Cleat. She briefly recalled her fathers description of him "Bald as a neep bit no as clever, poor thing".

She started bolt upright as a tap came on the door, "Janet, Janet, you there? Janet…"

Janet remained still, never moving a muscle…she was in a state of shock from the day's events and could not cope with any more …

"Janet Forsyth, speak to me you whalp….I ken you are there."

"Oh my god, is it you Ben, is it really you, I'm not dreaming am I, tell me I'm not dreaming, this morning I really did see you…"

A key rattled in the lock and the cell door creaked open, adjusting his eyes to the darkness Ben ran across to Janet.

"Oh my god Benjamin Garrioch,…Benjamin,… Ben, how on earth…"

"Shhhh, questions must wait…I'm alive and as real as this damned awful smelly cell. I'm here to take you away. No more talk, just follow me and do everything I say…
Someone behind lit a candle and passed it to Ben. "Put on this old breex and jacket, pull the cap down over your face and hang on to me like you are a young boy who has been all night in the pub and drunk too much rum… seriously… our lives depend on it."

Without the benefit of a hug or a kiss Ben took her arm and led her back along dark stone corridors, through a large cold room where most of her clothing had previously been removed, leaving her with nothing but an old canvas coverall for warmth, maximum degradation was order of the day for convicts.
Two men lay on the floor, Janet turned and looked at Ben, "I never touched them, Ewen's rum is the best rum north

of Edinburgh, they accepted our gift readily. Sleep well boys", Ben grinned, "you'll need every help God can provide to talk yourselves out of this one."

Janet could see nothing of where she was being led as the tweed cap was firmly pulled down over her ears and face, however the comfort of Jaimie was all she needed and clung on tightly. They staggered up the cobbled street skirting a group of drunken men. "Say nothing, keep your head down" Ben whispered as they approached "Hands full with your young shipmate their sailor", shouted a jovial voice as they approached, "want a dram" another offered a bottle as they passed.

"Young boys only learn the hard way, he's needing no more tonight, thank you, I can guarantee he'll no want another rum for weeks", the laugher faded behind as they staggered on across the town.

A mile or so out beyond Kirkwall's town boundary the countryside darkness was engulfing, however still playing the part of Bens drunken friend Janet kept quiet. A flickering light eventually guided them towards the door of an old barn. A horse snorted as Janet was hauled up onto the back of a cart beside two other men who said very little other than "Hi... made it then". She was cold and clung to Ben praying this dream would have a good end. "Keep yourself down under the canvas, the excise man will be out on the prowl on a bonny night like this" Ben said, "I'll sit up front in me Navy uniform and help to ward off awkward questions should we be stopped. Remember, there is a long way to go yet, whatever happens please play the part of the young drunk sailor, it works most every time".

"You should ken Ben me boy" the old tar sat beside him quipped and nudged him in the ribs.

Every bump and turn was painful as the cart rumbled its way through the countryside, Janet's emaciated body bounced and landed painfully on the hard wooden floor for what seemed like many miles. "You all right under that canvas back there Jan?" someone shouted after she had inadvertently let go a groan having being flung across the width of the cart.

My name isn't Jan she thought, I have always hated Jan, especially from people I don't know. Shortening someone's name is rude. "Oh what am I ranting to myself about, these guys are risking life and limb to save me." she whispered, horrified how her mind was wandering and confused. Janet tried to focus on here and now; she knew it had been at least two days since she ate anything, a mere drink of water would be welcome. She felt very light-headed and had a weird sensation of floating above the whole scene and watching it play out before her eyes.
"I can feel pain as I am heaved around the back of this cart, so it can't be a dream" she thought.
"If this is for real there will be a hunt for me in the morning, where can we hide, where are they taking me? Better bruised and breext than dead" she comforted herself aloud and wrapped the blanket tight around her shoulders ready for the next bump.

Coming to a halt as morning daylight was arriving, everything took on a yellowish hue, Janet peeped out from under the tarpaulin and watched Ben slip a few coins to the young carriage driver. He looked much more friendly than his voice last night she thought. A nod was the only

acknowledgement that passed between them as he jumped down from the cart and unhitched the sweating horse.
Ben helped Janet down from the cart and led her across to a bench outside the large stone building. "Deer Sound" she said quietly looking across the bay, "I've been here before, many years ago"

"Look yonder Janet, our transport to another life" Jaimie was pointing across the sparkling water where a large ship lay at anchor in the middle of the bay.
"Recognize that boat Janet?" Ben asked lifting damp matted hair from her cheek.

"Well I'll be damned, of course, the Emily Jane"

Janet could see men up the mast and out on the yards making ready for sea.
At the waters edge a recognizable Captain Mac was standing, looking up at the arrival party. Two men were up to their knees in the water holding on to a dinghy, patiently waiting. "Good to see you again Lady Pilot" he shouted, "get your arse down here before the tide turns".

A hearty breakfast of boiled eggs, bere bannoks, cheese and milk was set before Janet and Ben as they sat side by side at the captain's table, so close you couldn't slide a sheet of paper between them. "This easterly wind will see us in Liverpool before the end of the week" captain Mac began as his voice disappeared amongst the rattle of winches and clumping of boots across the wooden deck above.

Ben and Janet talked non-stop until the sun set on another day and Orkney was left in their wake far behind.
Ben explained that on that fateful day many summers ago when he, his brother Davo and Greetan Tam went missing, a fog had engulfed them out west of Noup, a strong ebb tide had taken the boat far offshore and the sight of land had been lost. The sky eventually cleared into a fine day and despite being many miles from home they decided to dip their lines for a fish. However, no sooner had they started to catch some big haddock, sails appeared over the horizon, a naval ship flying the English flag. They had no chance of out-running the warship and were pressed into Naval Service. They spent the following years crossing many seas and fighting many battles. The three of them had even been across the vast ocean to the west and visited the New World. Davo had jumped ship there and Ben explained that he had been sorely tempted to join him, however knew his beloved Janet was waiting in Westray and was determined to make his way home to find her again.
Ben told them of how he had been recognized and appreciated as a hardworking able crewman and earned himself an early discharge from service.

"It turns out there are other Orkney men in the English Navy and three were paid off with me in Wick only three days ago and I was making best haste to find passage home to Westray.
Oh Janet, my world collapsed when I wandered into that cathedral building; the maelstrom of depravity chanting for the burning of a witch was bad enough, but then I saw you, shackled in front of that blood-thirsty crowd of maniacs. That was more scary than being boarded by the entire Spanish navy."

"You've been on my mind constantly since the day I was taken from Orkney. Oh God just think... I might have missed you had it not been raining; we stopped to find shelter in the Cathedral and light our pipes."

Ben looked into Janet's eyes, and a tear ran down his cheek.

"Witch, witch, hang the bitch, they were chanting. It was like a lightning bolt hit me...I couldn't believe what I was seeing...I leaped towards the crowd who were all back on to us, arms in the air. My friend Joe and the other two sailors held me back or I would have been in there, fists flying. They were right of course, that would have caused more problems than I could have possibly hoped to solve had I been allowed to charge in to your rescue at that point...I would never have even have made it past the first row...
I can't imagine how difficult this whole thing has been for you Janet; these last few days appears to be the culmination of many years of persecution and mental hell you have suffered out there alone. How can you ever forgive me for not being with you to support."

"It has been a very difficult period indeed Ben....promise to fill you in with all the gory details in due course. It was not your fault you were unable to be there...however you came back and found me and that's what matters. Please tell me first though, how did you manage to organize all this rescue thing?"

Well...it took me less than one minute of time watching the deteriorating situation there at the great door of the cathedral to decide on what to do next; we had to return post haste to the Ale house on the harbour front."

"Ben, how could you go to the tavern, when you knew I was in such desperation, was a jug of ale more important?"

"Sorry lass, I tease...Naa, not for the ale, I went back to speak to captain Mac whom I knew was there, not one hour before, we had yarned over a jar of ale. He told me how you had saved his boat and crew from certain disaster and having now effected repairs to his rig was lying in Deersound hoping to sail west on the morning ebb home to Liverpool. He had no idea you had been arrested since they had moved the boat to the Mainland for repairs. I figured this could provide an ideal escape route and he readily agreed to assist, given his huge debt of gratitude he would have waited for many tides for us to arrive."

A couple of hours after you had been led from that dreadful court my old pal Ewen from the tavern made his way to the cell they call Marwicks Hole and supplied the guards outside with more ale and rum than they had ever encountered in one sitting. Job done. Once these poor sods were asleep we were able to pick up the keys and walk in....you know the rest."

"What can I say..... Captain Mac....Ben......oh my God." Janet wrapped her arms tightly around her beloved as tears rolled down her cheeks.

"Benjamin" captain Mac quietly interjected, "I believe you told me there was something you were going to ask Janet?"

He stood up, the gently rolling deck made him stagger a little as he looked out the port, obviously satisfied with the boats position and progress he sat down again. Janet thought the past few days had taken their toll on captain Mac and she hoped any revelation that was obviously coming was not going to involve the captain asking her to assist with any underlying health problems, she was feeling a bit queasy with the ships motion as it was.

"Ah yes" Ben replied "Indeed so, I need no reminder. I really wanted this moment to be somewhere romantic; Grobust beach on a sunny day or even the barn at Vere...however to be sailing south with the only person in the world I have ever loved in our privately chartered sailing ship will suffice.
I also have a highly qualified witness...I think this just about fits the bill!"

"Witness. Witness for what?" Janet asked with suspicion, flicking her eyes back and fore between the two gentlemen sat at the table.

Ben cleared his throat, gently took hold of Janet's hands and held her for a full two minutes, gazing into her eyes.

"Janet, I have loved you since the day we first met in Westray and I want to spend the rest of my life with you" His voice dropped into a whisper "and of course share you with our many children should we be fortunate".

Janet looked deeply into Bens dark blue eyes and her thoughts made her blush.

"Will you marry me Janet?"

"Oh Ben this all sounds much too like a dream and I fear I might wake up soon. You deserve better than me. I can never return to Westray. We can never be together"

"We have so much to catch up on Janet; it's a big world out there and this is only the start of the rest of our lives together. Remember those long winter nights we cuddled up together in the barn, sharing dreams of leaving the isles and making our fortunes? I haven't yet told you about the house I purchased in a bonny peedie toon in the south of England, its small but it's mine. There is a shop attached, on which I have first refusal to purchase once the old lady retires. It maybe doesn't sound much, but it means we can be together.
Will you join me Janet?"

"Ben, my very special Ben, you are the most amaising person in the world. Of course, I will."

Grasping the back of the wooden armchair, Captain Mac swung himself around the table and selected a bottle of Port and three glasses from the well-stocked cabinet. "I have been keeping this expensive reserve for a special occasion and believe there can be little more special than this. I have witnessed your vows, which I deem to be most sincere and you will be aware, as captain of the Emily Jane I am qualified to conduct on-board marriages...."

"With all due respect Captain I am exhausted, It's been a very long week, year, life.... I need time to adjust and must think this through." Looking into Bens eyes Janet worried the dream might end.
"However, you needn't delay the Port."

THE END

Some words are English with an accent, some words are Orcadian....

Foosty	-	damp and smelly.
Noust	-	stone or earth build boat nest.
Vooan	-	nagging/preaching/moaning.
Debblin'	-	dunking a jug into.
Poots	-	sulk.
Skited	-	slid.
Flix	-	fright/to frighten.
Thoo	-	you.
Thee	-	you'r
Thoo'll	-	you will.
Ken	-	know.
Peedie	-	small.
Teen	-	taken.
Thaft	-	seat (in a dinghy)
Morn	-	tomorrow.
Stooks	-	oat sheaves stood up in fours to dry,
Nort	-	north
Fattie cutties	-	griddle scones.
Wir	-	our.
Lugs	-	ears.
I doot	-	I am afraid.
Gisened	-	dried out.
Ceuth	-	coalfish.
Neeps	-	turnips.
Plantiquoy	-	small walled garden,
Simmans	-	straw rope.
Mither	-	mother.
Kist	-	wooden chest.
Skerry	-	tiny island/rocks.
Tanglie man	-	man who gathers seaweed/kelp off the beach.
Mallimack	-	seagull (fular).
Spoots	-	rasorfish/clam.
Scorries	_	seagulls (general).
Knowe	-	hillock (often with trowes living inside).
Belkie	-	rotten fish.
Haak	-	scrounger.
Beating flux	-	flailing arms against ones side,
Buxan	-	soaking wet.
Slok	-	put out (the flame),
Monkeys fist	-	fancy plaited rope ball.
Breex	-	trousers.
Bolster	-	double-size pillow.
Mither	-	mother.
Neepian	-	knitted headscarf/hood.
Whalp	-	brat (puppy in Shetland).
Breext	-	sore, tired mu

Printed in Poland
by Amazon Fulfillment
Poland Sp. z o.o., Wrocław